THIS MAY BE KEPT
**7 DAYS ONLY**
IT CANNOT BE RENEWED OR TRANSFERRED

D1301662

# WATER IN DARKNESS

## Daniel Buckman

Washington Free Public Library
120 East Main St.
Washington, IA 52353

**AKASHIC BOOKS**
**NEW YORK**

*The author wishes to acknowledge his debt of gratitude to his editor, Katherine Drayne Blount.*

This is a work of fiction. All names, characters, places, and incidents are the product of the author's imagination. Any resemblance to real events or persons, living or dead, is entirely coincidental.

Published by Akashic Books
©2001 Daniel Buckman

Skyline illo and art assistance by Thomas Alberty
Digital imaging by Richard P. Waltman

ISBN: 1-888451-19-X
Library of Congress Catalog Card Number: 00-112241
All rights reserved
First printing
Printed in Canada

Akashic Books
PO Box 1456
New York, NY 10009
Akashic7@aol.com
www.akashicbooks.com

*For Marie A. Buckman*
*and Rebecca S. Staton*

6114101 B41 21001/1100

For God maketh my heart soft, and the almighty troubleth me: Because I was not cut off before the darkness, neither hath he covered the darkness from my face.

*—Job 23: 16-17*

**T**he C-130 gained altitude out of Honduras so suddenly that the soldiers reeled in the seats where they sat facing each other in long rows. They vomited bile into MRE ration bags. They swallowed plug tobacco and doubled over, coughing dryly. Their jungle fatigues were kneeless and sweat black and without crotches. PFC Russell Fredericks fell forward and busted the piss-tube from the airplane wall before landing face down among the muddy boots of the soldiers. They laughed at this chubby hairlip from Tennessee where he lay helpless and pissing while the airplane held a steep northeast by southwest. He flailed his arms like a cartoon idiot and slid backward on his chest, followed by the rivulet of a hundred soldiers' urine floating cigarette butts and tobacco twists. The men cussed him in a babel of accents and lifted their shineless boots.

Fredericks' squirting penis dangled when he knelt, the legs of his fatigues black. The airplane banked through a wall of dark clouds and knocked him back down. He spat, his lips glazed with urine. The soldiers laughed and shot burning matches at his cushy backside or threw what they had in their hands. Wads of gum. Snuff tins. Pieces of ham and chicken loaf from their rations. Harold Felder, a stringy black from Miami, whipped red welts into his ass with a length of knotted parachute chord. The rest waited with tired faces to rig up for the jump back into Fort Bragg.

Crack the cracker motherfucker, Felder said.

That's it, said a yellow-skinned black named Pickens. Ain't no joking when we ain't toking.

Jack Tyne sat on the web seats next to Jimmy Wilder, the short Virginian the NCO's called Nub. Wilder was livid, rolling his eyes like a mad preacher when Corporal Keller jumped up and pushed Fredericks back down into his piss wake after the airplane straightened itself at cruising altitude. Keller was a handsome lawyer's son from Pittsburgh who had gone to Rutgers on a wrestling scholarship and flunked out. Jack hated him, but they'd been together since the first day of boot camp, even before the barbers shaved their heads and the drill sergeants boxed up their civilian clothes to send home. He smiled at Jack and gave him the peace sign. Wilder shook his head and stared out the window at the sky flowing past. *Only the maniacs are alive here,* Jack thought, *only they can stand to run things.*

The soldiers howled and congratulated Keller with back slaps and high fives for prolonging the floor show. Two boy-faced lieutenants looked on with disgust before laughing themselves when Fredericks stood with his pants around his ankles, looking like he'd wandered in from an overturned bus of idiots. Sergeant Nien, pock-faced and two months off drill sergeant's duty, ordered Fredericks to leave his pants undone and jam his thumb into his mouth. After a five-thousand count he was to take it from his wet lips and proclaim loudly that he was a shitbird. Keller was stung, red-faced, huffing like a scorned woman at being outdone by Nien. Jack Tyne and Wilder lit cigarettes while Fredericks affirmed his new name every five seconds.

I'm a shitbird.

I'm a shitbird.

Look at Keller, Wilder said. I bet he feels worse than a dog kicked at suppertime.

I went through boot camp with him, Jack said. He was the first of all the assholes to start talking like the drill sergeants. There was this kid Miller with a big head and small girl hands and Keller gave him hell for sixteen weeks just like the drills did. You'd hear Miller crying in the latrine at night and then he tried to kill himself with a disposable razor. I don't know what Keller's going to do when he gets out.

He's a lifer, Jacky. We'll come back in twenty years after he's a retired first sergeant and see him driving a taxicab from division out to all the titty bars. He'll be telling the new joes how hard it all was back in 1987.

Keller pointed at Fredericks where he sat nervously sucking his teeth, black from snuff. Keller was trying to get their attention with his game-show-host face before slapping Fredericks upside his head and telling him to close his mouth. Fredericks rubbed the back of his neck and held his peter through his pants like a boy who had to piss during a church service.

Hey Jacky, Keller said. Who told this shitbird there was anybody who wanted to see his teeth?

Jack smiled vaguely. Wilder gave Keller the finger without even looking at him.

Buddy fuckers, Keller yelled. You buddy fucking sons of bitches.

You know, Jack, Wilder said. You never get to pick who you spend your life seeing.

Jack pointed at Fredericks with his tired eyes.

Or what the hell you look like, he said.

I know it ain't nice, but Fredericks' face kind of invites it all. He looks like the offspring of cousins. But Keller is an asshole.

And he thought he was going to see a war in Honduras, Jack said.

Just to think.

The jump masters stood barrel-chested beside the jump doors and cursed the men to their feet. The smokers took final drags from cigarettes and held the smoke until none came out. The outboard seats were locked upright and the inboard seats followed suit. Parachutes packed in green nylon were ferried down the rows of pimple-faced soldiers; the yellow static lines were bound to the pack trays by rubberbands and the boys were careful not to mess them. Reserve chutes like couch pillows were passed nervously along. Jack Tyne knew the reserves would be useless; the jump altitude back into Fort Bragg was only seven hundred feet and they would not have time to fully deploy. The battalion commander—Old Buck they called him—wanted to simulate the conditions of a combat jump because an occasion for training could never be wasted. When it's for real, he said, you don't want your balls hanging too long in the sky. He had promised the boys of the 3/504th Parachute Infantry a fight in Honduras with the fury of a minister testifying grace. Many thought the old man with steel eyes half hidden away in the deep seams of his face wanted to avenge the American dead he had seen in Vietnam when he led a platoon from the 101st Airborne through the A Shau Valley. But no fight along the Honduran-Nicaraguan border came to pass and he would retire at the end of the year without hope of getting his full bird. When all of the live ammunition and grenades were returned, the old man sulked darkly, exuding the inconsolable sadness of a man passed over who knows that all a retired warrior can do on the outside is sell real estate or teach high school history. But his soldiers had fun, joking and calling the absent Nicaraguans Juan Cong, the killers of rum bottles and bags of Panama Red. They jeered the jungle and the orange frogs and claimed that they feared no evil in the valley of the shadow of death because they were the meanest motherfuckers in the valley. They acted like Hollywood actors in every movie they had ever seen about the Vietnam War, sketching peace signs on their helmet covers, talking about The Man, playing air guitar with the butts of their M-16 rifles to ill-hummed riffs of Jimi Hendrix, once a paratrooper like themselves.

Wilder adjusted the sizing straps on his chute back to fit his small body. His teeth were crooked and gapped, yellow from too long in the field.

I'm glad I'm out next month, he said to Jack. Keller's going to be impossible with him having Honduras. I just can't stand to hear none of his bullshit anymore.

Jack inspected his parachute without any idea of what he was looking for. He wiped a muddy bootprint off its nylon cover.

Keller can't have what didn't happen, he said. We sat around down there scaring each other with dead snakes.

That doesn't mean nothing to a jerk-off like Keller. He was there and they let him load his rifle and lead a patrol. He'll be telling that to every new guy this year.

What do you think gets a guy started telling the same story? Jack said.

He don't have shit else to say. The army is already the high point of his life at twenty-one. I think once an idiot gets started on something, he more or less sticks to it his whole life.

I guess.

There ain't nothing to guess, Jacky. Back home, there's this old drunk named Larry Ray who lives in the trailer park and drinks one of them big jugs of vodka every couple days. You always see him staggering to town every Monday and Wednesday and Friday and sometimes Saturday if it's cold out. He tells the guy at the Piggly Wiggly about how he don't call blacks niggers. No, sir, he says. He calls them South American Dignitaries like Sanders did in the navy. Nobody knows what he means let alone who Sanders is. But we think he might be the dumb son of a bitch who once talked him up from a barstool and made him think he was a comedian.

Jack nodded while the sunlight strafed through the windows.

You can't give an idiot the time of day, Wilder said. If you listen once, you're fucking everybody that's ever got to watch his mouth move.

Jack and Wilder helped each other into their parachutes, then fought to keep their shoulders square from the weight of the overstuffed rucksacks hanging before their legs. They waited to be inspected. Jack steadied himself with a hand against the insulated wall of the airplane, counting five months until discharge.

Fredericks was still unrigged and lay wide-eyed on a pile of unused reserve parachutes. Jack knew his type—slow, mulish, looking at a future of moving between welfare lines and county jobs and cheap rents. He was the fat boy who made the drill sergeants at Fort Benning love their duty. They sought his kind out that first day of boot camp as if he were the finest piece of meat on the platter, calling him before the formation of scrotum-headed boys and declaring that the best part of him ran down his momma's leg. They jammed the brims of their Smokey-the-Bear hats into his bovine face and left them there for twelve weeks, hoping to run him AWOL from their army. But Fredericks endured, his destitute imagination never knowing the difference unless the drill sergeant was black; most of them cussed him with his own accent. Jack figured guys like him stuck around for the chow that came hot and regular, chili-mac and Wonder Bread.

Sergeant Nien, wild-eyed for a drink, crossed his arms and tilted his head down to see into Fredericks' face. Perhaps it was a vision of some hill girl gotten in the cab of a pickup truck that was making Fredericks' feet tremble. Jack elbowed Wilder and pointed for him to look.

Fredericks, Sergeant Nien said. His crazy boozer's face twitched grimly.

Fredericks looked up with the graceless eyes of a cow.

Yes, Sergeant, he said.

You get a good rest?

Yes.

You feel like you're ready for the jump?

I sure do.

We have a parachute all ready for you, Nien said. But only if you're rested.

This one? Fredericks said.

You don't mind, do you?

Hell no, Sergeant. I volunteered to be airborne.

I'm really happy you're a man of his word.

My daddy says that all a man has is his word and his balls and that he shouldn't go breaking them for nobody.

That's some good advice. Uncle Sugar does not want anybody making his daddy ashamed.

Damn, Sergeant, you even remind me of my daddy.

When Fredericks stooped down for the parachute, Nien fetched him a kick to his backside, once again laying him among the boots of the soldiers. Lemmings, the lanky machine gunner from third squad, pulled him up by his neck in time to keep Felder from stumbling over his head. Nien smirked and made his way up the aisle to inspect parachutes. Keller's rat eyes followed him with jealous respect, as if this were the man he knew he wanted to become.

Get rigged, you moron, Lemmings said. Nien ain't had a drink in twelve days and if you make him any more pissed off, I'll blindside you myself.

I didn't know which parachute was mine, Fredericks said.

Well, said Lemmings, there ain't a wrong one.

Wilder was shaking his head while he held up his

rucksack to have its lowering line inspected by Sergeant Tommy Brown, a man who got so drunk on Saturday night that he gave himself two IVs every Sunday morning to rehydrate himself, watching professional wrestling on a black-and-white TV as the bags drained into his thick arms. He looked over his shoulder at Jack.

Good thing we didn't fight them people, he said. Half of these fools are just here because the factories closed back home, the other half are only wanting to talk shit. We'd a died in place.

You really think so, Jack said.

Shit.

Jack sat with the others, a parachute and rucksack across his knees. He buried his head in his folded arms atop his reserve, smelling the putrid breath from a soldier's nicotine cough. He closed his eyes and feigned sleep.

*There are nights when I fool myself that I can remember my father. It's mostly the small things I pretend I once saw. The worn heels of his work boots. The way his eyes would half close when he drew his cigarette. The soap smell of his neck when he held me on his shoulders to watch two buck deer duel on a bluff above the Watega River. I even stare unblinking at the cinder blocks of the barracks wall until I see him telling me things about the world. He explains to me that where there is true sadness, no consolation is possible. His face always shows great concern, as if hoping that in my youth I will understand his wisdom and experience. I listen intently to my own delusion, even on nights when his mouth moves without sound.*

*I have tricks I do when I cannot imagine him talking to me anymore. I close my eyes and open them quickly. I shake my head hard with my eyes open. But he never returns. He dies again among the wet ruins of Hue City the way I have always seen him when I cannot lie anymore to myself that he might have been a father who did something that warranted a memory. His wet boots protrude from the burst concrete; the rats climb about the slabs like children at play. He is dead by a gut-*

shot, his PX wristwatch smashed. All of the dead marines wear the same PX wristwatch and the few that remain ticking are stolen by smiling children in pointed hats. The dropped arms bounce lifelessly on the broken glass.

Number one, the children giggle. Number one dead joes.

In my sister's last letter she wrote for the first time of her sadness about his death. I never knew Gina thought of him. She was always my brown-eyed sister so beautiful too young, taking the stares of men as if a statue before she was thirteen years old. Our father was only a young marine in a picture on the television set, his face phony grim. Our mother took it away when she married Donny, the man who stayed too fat for the draft until the Vietnam War was over, his face scarred from bad acne, his clothes smelling of the dog food he made at General Foods on the afternoon shift. It was like our mother killed him for the second time, because he became nothing but a VA headstone, the flat sheet of bronze, and she asked with her cold eyes that we call this fat man father. But Gina wrote that there are many things a woman cannot even begin to know without her father's love.

Her vague words haunt me because I never meant to watch her and Donny for so long on those nights. I even held a tire iron against my leg, feeling the coldness of the metal, telling myself that this would be the night I would use it, open his curly head like an egg and kill him atop her. But I did nothing and only watched them through the cracked door of her bedroom, the darkness wet beyond the window, the rain lulled as if a calmed hysteric. Then she was forever atop him, so much like lovers, his calloused fingers about her slender hips, working her against his hardness, until embracing Gina to lick the undersides of her breasts. She was not fifteen. But I tell myself over and over that I saw her child's face die when she never really had one.

Our mother was awake like me. She heard those nights the way I saw them. The rain blowing against the bungalow windows in tiny squalls. Their breath sucking like the wind in the trees. But I never meant to watch so long and I wonder if our mother meant to listen.

* * *

A frayed light leaked through the airplane windows when the jump masters ordered the soldiers to their blistered feet. The boys moaned sadly while they helped each other up with outstretched hands across the aisles. Rucksacks swung and busted shins. Wilder spat and murmured that his time was way too short in the army for a jump to break his back. They hooked their static lines to the cables above, halved the slack, and held it tightly, checking rucksack lowering-lines with hard tugs. The RTOs sighed from the weight of radios. The machine gunners examined the rigging of their weapons, stroking the black gunmetal like beloved pets. They all rocked back and forth with the maneuverings of the crazed pilot.

The jump masters, shrouded in the red light from the cabin, pushed open the doors and kicked down the jump platforms, the wind forcing their pants tightly about their thighs. The cold dark air drenched the airplane and woke Jack and a hundred others from their thoughts. The jump masters hung from the doors, looking for the leading edge of the drop zone, only their boot heels and fingers visible. The soldiers stomped like straining horses and chanted for death to come quickly if death were to come at all.

When the safeties pulled the jump masters from the doors, they straightened their kevlar helmets upon their heads and gave the thirty-second warning by hand signal. The first jumper, a soft-faced lieutenant named Rhodes, took his position in the door. His knees trembled. The safety held the yellow static line behind his back.

The green light popped and the soldiers yelled that the bullshit must stop. The jump masters howled go and Rhodes went. The stick of jumpers shuffled to the door and reeled from the cruel blast of wind. They handed off their static lines with extreme care, their bodies suicidally beautiful as they walked into the blast and cursed the souls of the men who led them. Jack followed Wilder and closed his eyes after handing off his line, and soon there was nothing below his feet but the darkness.

The night was sodden and cool when Jack Tyne pitched his rucksack over the gate of the canopied deuce-and-a-half. He jumped down into the sterile quiet of Fort Bragg, the painted rocks marking formation areas, the raked dirt beneath manicured bushes. He blew cold while he slung his rifle and searched for Wilder in the line of soldiers filing along the regimental street, their faces whisker-dark, orange from cigarette embers.

Felder and Pickens shot hot butts at a fat motor sergeant who stood on the running board of an idling deuce. His uniform was starched; his stomach bulged against his blouse. He ordered the lazy grunts to stop dick-dancing and shag ass off his trucks. The cigarette butts bounced off his head. Passing soldiers called him a cake-eater, a pogue, a dirty leg motherfucker.

Who did that? he said. He brushed the singe out of his hair.

Nobody here but us niggers, said Felder and Pickens. Not a soul.

Jack leaned forward from the weight on his back while the fat sergeant was barraged with hot butts, the sparks flying like the wake from tracers. The barracks buildings were built of cinder blocks, rowed four deep, as if a hundred sets of clean teeth. Wilder and Keller were at ease on the rocks of the formation area with the forming company, wiping grime from their lips, scratching bug bites into runny welts. Keller held a Zippo against the asshole of farting Gruber and swore blue flames would appear; none did even though Gruber's forehead was red from straining. Wilder looked like he would sit down with his face in his hands if somebody let him. Jack fell in beside Cassiday, a buck-toothed kid from Kansas who shit on the latrine floor whenever he got drunk. His eyelids were pus bags from some bug bite and hung like awnings overfilled with rain.

Do my eyes look real bad, Jacky? Cassiday said.

They sure the fuck do, Jack said.

Really?

All fucked up.

First Sergeant Johnny Johnson took his place before Bravo Company on a cement pallet formed into the grass. He was a black man, tall and hard like a framing nail, his face pockmarked with bullet scars from the Ia Drang Valley. The combat infantrymen's badge and master jumpwings were stitched above his left pocket, the ranger tab on his shoulder. Behind him were a row of white crosses against the billet walls with the name of every AWOL and dope fiend and barracks thief he had ever sent to military prison. For six days the first sergeant patrolled the Honduran frontier with his soldiers, and his jungle fatigues still bore a starch crease, his boots brush-shined. *Cleanliness in the face of squalor, men, he would say. That is all a soldier can offer this world of pig-fucking civilians.* He laughed in the faces of the young blood officers who were sure they would fight the Sandanistas, as if he knew the operation was a dog-and-pony show ordered by President Reagan himself. *A gang of spics won't fight for anything except whores and drugs, he said. But Charlie Cong would have killed half you fist-fuckers the first day out. You would be dead, still trying to drop your cocks and find your socks.* The first sergeant consulted his wristwatch with hard glances and waited for his men to form.

Two new guys from the replacement depot walked down the barracks stairway. They were freshly hatched from boot camp and jump school at Fort Benning, fitted in new fatigues full of pocket strings. Jack watched them take slow steps as if walking across ice. Bravo Company howled and whistled, called places in the love train they promised would run all night long. There was a lanky white boy with soft gray eyes and willowy legs who sauntered rather than walked, a stigma he never knew he had until the first day of boot camp when the drill sergeants asked him if he joined the Army to fight or fall in love. A black kid followed him, scowling and eyeing all as if he'd killed up close with a zip gun, even bitten off noses in night fights on the wintry streets of Detroit.

The first sergeant called the company to attention with gravel dead eyes and never once looked up from his wristwatch. One hundred and fifty boots locked heels in uncanny unison. He studied his charges, not liking half of what he saw. This motley of drawling Klansmen and tattooed skinheads and black gangbangers from the west side of all places and Mexicans raised in the border barrios where the sunrises looked like graffiti. Every one of them was unfit for real work and wore a smirk that no amount of pain could wipe away. He pointed into the formation with a karate chop where the soldiers fought the desire to scratch mosquito bites.

You pissants have three minutes to baptize these men and make them real paratroopers, he said. Are you all clear?

The soldiers screamed that they were very clear.

Prepare to baptize, he said.

Many hooted the rebel yell as their doomed forebears had done across a wheat field so long ago.

Baptize. The first sergeant's hand came down with violence.

The formation area became a stampede and the new soldiers were set upon by the feral herd. Jack and Wilder stood back, as if wrapped in an odd nimbus of calm. Keller led a wave of men against the pretty boy and soon held his frail body high like a coffin. The soldiers took turns slapping his stomach red. He offered no resistance and they struck him harder for it.

The black stood his ground and swung first against Fredericks, the punch solid upon his jaw followed by a clean uppercut. Fredericks reeled and spat blood. The black kicked against his head when he came to his knees and sent him back flat. He was trampled by his avengers and they circled the black, unsure of how to bay him. He guarded his face with his fists and punched coolly, sending three to the gravel before going down beneath a dog pile. He kicked and gouged and bit all things within reach. A soldier named Rawlins with a bad tick rolled from the pile holding his testicles.

The nigger bit my cock, he said.

Gruber with his crooked eyetooth ran to the barracks wall and turned on the water spigot. Keller led his herd toward it with the pretty boy high on their hands. They banged his head against the wall. His eyes swam, his tongue lolled from his mouth. His new fatigues were heavy with water. Keller and Gruber held him upside down by his ankles. Soldiers huddled five deep and peered over shoulders to see, fighting one another for a better view.

Shake the cherry, Gruber, Keller said. Get the water down into his nose.

The cocksucker won't keep still, Gruber said.

I got his head, said an ugly voice. I got his head right here.

The first sergeant looked skyward and yelled that it was finished and it was. The soldiers filed back to their platoons. The pretty boy rose dazed and coughing from the harsh flow of water. He took a short step before collapsing into the puddled grass, then stood again, his eyes crossed and swelling badly. No soldier offered him aid because he had refused to fight. He was now marked weak and the weak were useless, and Jack Tyne knew that there was no future in helping a marked man. It was only a matter of weeks before they came for him in the barracks dark and beat him until he went AWOL.

The black jumped to his feet, picked up his maroon beret, and brushed it off against his leg. The soldiers from his new platoon cheered him for his toughness. There was no mark upon his face nor would one ever come to it. Even his bloody-nosed victims shook his hand.

There's one tough nigger, Keller said. I wish we had him in our platoon.

Wilder looked at him and forced laughter as if to keep from crying.

I wouldn't go saying that too loud, he said.

What am I saying that's bad, Keller said. He's a tough nigger, ain't he?

Go on, Killer, yell it out. First Sergeant Johnson ain't heard what you have to say about his momma.

The orange-haired corporals Gilligan and Hoey of South Boston poured swallows of beer on the barracks hallway, then jigged new scuff marks into the brown tiles. Jimmy Cross waited by the broom closet for them to pass on into the night and find the road to the tavern. He held the mop in the ringer, the bucket water black as river mud. Cross had broken his ankle on a jump two months ago and had pins in his knee. The first sergeant turned him into a janitor until his medical profile expired and took him from the shame of light duty.

Cross kicked the bucket with his good leg when the Irish corporals walked down the stairs. The water lopped on the floor, thin puddles of filthy suds and pine oil. His cast was wrapped in a trash bag and he swung the mop head back over the tiles he had just cleaned.

Jack stood in the doorway of the room he shared with Keller. He slipped a clean sweatshirt over his head still wet from a cold barracks shower. Cross hobbled behind his mop and mouthed curses under his breath.

Go easy, Cross, Jack said.

I've mopped this son of a bitch nine times. You know that. Nine goddamned times.

Cross bent down to pull cigarette butts from the mop head.

Like it's my fucking fault for breaking a leg, he said. I ain't no pogue, Tyne. I never fell out of anything.

Jack watched Cross move the mop faster, almost stabbing the floor with it.

They've had me on detail every day since, Cross said.

They have, Jack said.

Jumping out of airplanes ain't natural. Anybody could break a leg. Even first sergeant. Even the shitting colonel. This will fuck me out of the sergeant's board. This could have happened to any of you.

But it was you, Jack said.

Cross grit his teeth and shook his head.

I ain't even started laying wax yet, he said. You know what these fuckheads will do then?

At least they're still pissing in the latrine.

The night's young, Tyne. And you guys got a four-day pass.

Jack lit Cross's cigarette with a match and walked down the hall. Soldiers too poor for the taverns and the clip joints and the trailer park brothels off post lazed in the rooms. They drank canned beer and sipped whiskey from pint bottles. He stood in the doorway of Wilder's NCO room with one hand on the knob and a cigarette in his mouth. Wilder coughed and packed an overnight bag, his body still filthy from the jungle though he was dressed in jeans and a clean mackinaw.

I'm getting away from these idiots, Jack Tyne, he said. They're already down in Gruber's room with a case of Busch and Keller's passing a fifth of Early Times.

Since when did you stop drinking? Jack said.

That ain't it. I don't want to listen to them later. The howling and Keller wandering around with his jaw stuck out and wanting to wrestle third platoon. Not tonight. I'm getting me a room at the Fayetteville Motor Lodge and eating pizza until I forget my name.

Jack sat on the bunk and laughed at his friend.

They aren't going to give you a room smelling like that, he said.

I'll pay them double. Why don't you come on and we'll go halves.

I got to save my money for discharge, Jack said. I don't know what kind of home I have to go back to.

There isn't a shitface up and down this hallway who knows that. We're rolling the dice that the people back home will treat us like the heroes we ain't. Why don't you come on?

I can't.

Anders is on CQ and you know that dumbass don't care if they get drunk and go after that new kid again. He should have taken a swing or something. Keller's convinced he's a faggot. You know how they ran Kirkau AWOL last year.

Kirkau didn't have any business coming here.

They didn't even know if he was gay or not.

The barracks has its own law, Jack said.

With talk like that, you better get down to Gruber's room.

I don't see you sticking around to guard him, Jack said.

Get out of here. I don't want to listen to you either.

Jack walked off smiling. In Felder's room lolled an arrangement of blacks who were drunk or becoming that way. Coal faces, tawny faces, all inhaling wisps of menthol smoke. They fought to laugh the loudest over raps about forcible sodomy and gut-shot cops. Felder raised his soused eyes when Jack passed the doorway and staggered to his feet with a bottle of Bacardi 151 in one hand. The new black sat against a wall locker, still in uniform. Pickens was barefoot on the bunk, rapping with the stereo.

Hey Jacky Tyne, said Felder. You feeling all-white tonight.

He extended the bottle to Jack but Jack waved it away with his hand.

Come on and have a drink, Felder said.

Jack met the new black's cold eyes.

No, he said.

I was telling my boys here that you ain't too proud to drink after a nigger, Felder said. None of them believe me. That's why I'm saying you're all-white.

Pickens reeled on the bunk, keeping rhythm with his hands tapping his knees.

This cracker just wants to drink before a nigger and spit in the backwash, he said. Then beat my old boy up. Lynch the poor nigger before he gets to talking with the other niggers. Say that's what you wanted to do, Jacky Tyne. The truth shall set you free.

First Sergeant gave the order, Jack said.

Shit cracker, said Pickens. That tom motherfucker has been in the army so long he's whiter than your momma.

Felder rolled his saucer eyes.

Who gave this punk-ass motherfucker the rum? he said.

Pickens blew smoke hard at Jack from where he lay on the bunk.

Don't worry, cracker, he said. We niggers learn in school just how far we can go.

Shut your mouth, Felder said. I told you Jacky Tyne's all-white.

That's about it, said Pickens.

Nobody knows what to do with a drunk nigger, Felder said.

Not even us niggers, Pickens said. You got any ideas, cracker?

Their laughter blared like police sirens when Jack left the doorway and headed for the far end of the hallway, down toward Gruber's room for a beer chilled on the window ledge and a mouthful of Early Times and the chain-smoking of Marlboro Reds.

The new boy had left his door wide open. He sat motionless on his bunk in GI-issue brown skivvies. His duffel bags were slumped against the wall. He held a cigarette between his fingers and drew it, his blue eyes swimming like tropical fish in an aquarium way too small. Jack Tyne knew that Bravo Company would never forgive a quiet boy with skinny legs and full lips for ending up in their ranks. The only question now was what night they would come for him. Jack figured this boy understood it by the way he stared at the white wall as if he could see beyond the cold cinder blocks.

When Jack turned to leave, the new boy looked at him and smiled around his cigarette, one eye swollen shut and blackening.

My name is Andrew Thomas, he said.

Jack Tyne. Where are you from, Thomas?

You can call me Andrew.

Nobody else will, Jack said.

I'm from a lot of different places, Jack. I enlisted in Boston.

Your folks there, Thomas?

I was just in college. I had a hard time paying attention to things.

I'm from Watega, Illinois, Jack said. Don't tell anybody else about having been in college.

Thomas nodded and smoked his cigarette as if a woman who knew she was being watched.

My mother lives in Chicago, he said. My father never came home from Vietnam.

Neither did mine. He died at Hue City.

My mother was pregnant with me, Thomas said.

Mine was with my sister, Jack said. I was barely one year old.

We have a lot in common then.

Jack hated him for saying that. Andrew Thomas was already run AWOL and slinking off post in the dark with a broken nose from being beaten with soap tied into socks. There was no point in knowing him.

It's strange, Jack, Thomas said. But I keep looking for him. This man who has never been more than a dozen pictures. I came here to find him even though I know he's nowhere to be found.

Mine's just a dead guy to me, Jack said.

Wouldn't you like to have known him?

I've gotten along fine without a father, Jack said.

Thomas offered Jack a cigarette but he said no with his hand.

You don't smoke, Jack, he said.

Too many already. You spend a lot of time here sitting around and waiting to go someplace else and wait.

Thomas nodded and looked at Jack with wet eyes.

The game of hating the new guy will end when more new guys come, Jack said.

I've made a terrible mistake, Thomas said. My father is not here.

No, Jack lied. The game has rules.

Jack turned away from this sad boy and walked off to where Cross was buffing the tiles to a high shine and dragging his gimp leg behind him. The garbage bag that covered his cast was splattered with wax. Jack headed for the cocktail party in Gruber's room where the laughter had already gained a vulgar pitch.

*How do you know of such love, Gina? Where have you seen it?*

*Maybe you thought he would save us, but even in dreams he is a dead man, capable of nothing, his mud wet fatigues making him heavier for the graves detail that pulls him from the rubble by his ankles. The rain flecks the moist blood on his stomach, red like the catsup spilled from the hot dogs at Saint Joe's picnic onto the guts of laughing fat men who drink beer with Father Stremkowski. They ask the graying priest how many trips around the beads he will take for eyeing your breasts with them. The father smiles like cracked glass, nodding instead of saying a word. When did you first know that so many men wanted to fuck you? Our father could have done nothing. He is even a burden to the marines who carry his corpse. They cuss the size of his shoulders. Why do we always get the big guys? they say. The men drop him without watching him fall on the cratered street. We ain't carrying no more dead motherfuckers, they say. He is now one in a long row of corpses, their pants undone to check their testicles before they died, as if the package must be secured for the other side. What is heaven but the longest of our wet dreams?*

**D**anny Morrison walked into the vacant lot beneath the dark girders of the Lake Street El. His body was lank and hard, warmed by a Marine Corps field jacket, his eyes like dirty bottle glass looking hard into the wet wind. He kept his hand pocketed, wrapped around a snub-nosed .38 as he searched Lake Street for the skinny black with the bum leg from being run over by a bus the night he came home from Vietnam. *That spic wanted to run down a nigger that night, wanted it like a million goddamned dollars.* The man cruised the silent dark in a rusted Delta 88 selling the void in a vial, and Morrison was feeling the twitch, the dull ache that never stayed dull. The Damen bus sped south without passengers down the cratered street; the exhaust hazed in the cold like fog on wide water.

Two blacks warmed their hands at an old oil drum that burned more garbage than wood. The flames drew and twisted while the sleet turned the vacant lots between the housing projects into mud flats. Morrison spat in the dark gutter water where a bloated pigeon moldered. He sipped from a pint of J&B to hold off his edge even though he knew it wouldn't work for long.

The men at the fire wore a motley of tattered suit jackets and wool coats and odd pieces of clothing stolen from homeless shelters. The tallest of the two was shod in toeless basketball shoes wound around with duct tape. He stomped his feet in the mud as if to warm them. His thick glasses were tied to his face with a bootlace and he waved Morrison over from the shadows of the El tracks. The other man was younger with bullet scars on both cheeks, perhaps shot by a .22 while he laughed big laughs.

Morrison came into the hoop of firelight, watching their hands, while the kid took a piece of burning cardboard from the fire and held it to an unlit cigarette butt in his mouth. The paper flared, embers fell from his face, and he spat the cigarette out on the ground, coughing wildly. His eyebrows were singed, his eyes red and soapy.

I told the kid about lighting a cigarette that way, Danny Irish, the tall black said. I told him just tonight, but he don't listen to nobody. Not to the police. Not even to niggers same as him.

The kid wiped his eyes and blinked and hacked wet. Morrison kept to the edges of the firelight. The snowy mud was marred by a hundred boot sizes.

You got a taste for James, Danny Irish? the tall black said.

Morrison tossed him what was left in the pint bottle. James uncapped it with his bony hand and drank back more than his share before the kid could see right. When the kid cleared his eyes with his hands, he grabbed at the Scotch like it was a basketball.

I won't do you wrong, James said.

The kid called him a motherfucker and took the bottle from his face. His eyes darted like a feral cat. James reeled back two steps and shook his head. Morrison looked around the corner of a windowless liquor store for the man's Delta 88, but saw only the snow-covered filth.

Where's your cop suit, Danny Irish, the kid said.

He ain't the police no more, James said.

The kid killed the bottle and sent it up toward the El tracks where pigeons whirred on the dripping girders.

Why ain't you the police no more? the kid said.

He just ain't, James said.

So he's down with the niggers? What is it the police say about us niggers—if we can't fuck it, steal it, or eat it, we break it.

Shut your mouth, James said.

Then what's he doing here? the kid said. I bet he's going after booty. Lake Street is full of whores even in the cold. There's even these niggers fresh out of the jailhouse who dress up like bitches and tie their dicks back between their legs.

Morrison palmed the pistol handle in his pocket, then fingered the trigger.

He ain't up in here after booty, James said.

Them whores get to fighting in the summer, the kid said. They slice each other with razor blades. One whore bit off another whore's nose just because she was high. Then some little nigger comes up and runs away with the nose after she spits it out.

That's some evil, James said. It's down there all by itself, up on two damned legs.

Danny Irish knows about that place, the kid said. I bet he got his booty for nothing when he was the police.

Morrison backed out of the firelight altogether. His shadow quaked on the weedy mud like fast water and then faded.

You like to fight? he said to the kid.

In the kid's eyes the fire was reflected twice and very small, and he put them into Morrison's.

Yes, he said.

James clapped his hands together for warmth.

If you like fighting, he said, you ain't like the rest of us. You're like Dracula or King Kong.

The kid spat into the fire and wiped his mouth.

You get that army coat from fighting, Danny Irish? he said.

Shit, James said. Danny Irish was a war hero in Vietnam before he became the police.

You were in Vietnam? the kid said.

Morrison nodded. The fire was dying down to hot red coals.

I see niggers walking around all day in coats like that, the kid said. They'll tell you they were in Vietnam, too. You ain't nothing but a crack-head ex-cop.

You better shut your mouth, James said.

You kill those gook motherfuckers the way you killed niggers around here? the kid said.

Tell him to be quiet, Morrison said.

James put his arm around the kid and tried muscling him away but the kid would have none of it. He pushed the skinny James off of him with one hand and sent him staggering through the bottle glass.

You going to shoot me? the kid said.

It's your call, Morrison said.

He won't look at me in the eyes and shoot me cold. He's too sad about fucking up his life to be mean anymore.

Get him out of here, Morrison said.

The problem with niggers, James said, is that they spend too much time listening to other niggers.

I've been shot before by a real killer, not a punk-ass glaze face, the kid said.

Morrison drew the pistol and leveled it at the kid where the pale shrouds of smoke rose from the barrel. He thumbed back the hammer and sighted the post on the young, scarred face. The kid was motionless, without expression, like he was carved from an ancient stone.

James ran off through the vacant lot all alone, high-stepping through the slag puddles. He fell to his knees three times before he reached the street. The kid pocketed his hands and walked backward from the fire, his cat eyes never leaving Morrison's until he stepped upon the street. Then he moved away, as if only out to walk among the gutted buildings on the West Side of Chicago still charred from riot fires now twenty years past. Morrison was fully in the darkness as the fire died to nothing and the metal violence of the Lake Street El passed over his head, sounding not unlike his own suicidal dreams.

*Morrison filed with the remains of his platoon through the Thouong Tu Gate at Hue while a twilight rain darkened the ruined Citadel. Phantom jets cut overhead, trailing their coarse sounds long seconds after passing off into the clouds gathering out west. He was only one marine among many marines, his jungle fatigues ripped by concertina wire and blood-flecked from the assault against the wall that morning. They passed bombed colonnades abandoned these two weeks after the North Vietnamese overran Hue in a night fog and shot shopkeepers dead in the streets. Their bodies lay prone in loose clothing, slumped upon rubble with open mouths, their filthy chattels still tied to backs gored by bayonets. Morrison was the new guy, only in-country for three weeks when the Tet Offensive started, and nobody would talk to him, as if the other marines begrudged him his survival because so many had died that day with only weeks left of their tours. He knew none of their names; they did not know his.*

*Half-naked children called to the marines like barking dogs. They ran barefoot, their skinny yellow bodies gimping legless on makeshift crutches. The marines looked on darkly as the kids panhandled them with hands missing fingers. They tossed the children C-Ration chocolate and canned peaches that wedged hard in the mud. Morrison saw the wall at the*

end of the street where the North Vietnamese relieved themselves during the long fight.

The clanking of tanks grew loud behind the platoon. The
gunnery sergeant, a rawboned Texan with a cheek full of plug
tobacco, ordered his marines to part in the street like the fabled
sea. The two tanks passed, laden with marines both wounded
and dying, while freaked corpsmen held plasma IVs tightly into
bloody forearms. The wounded were shirtless and mummified
in filthy bandages with their heads wagging off the sides of the
tanks. The children ran in the tracks the iron treads made in
the red dirt and begged blinded men with voices like sick cats.

Rain peened off the sergeant's steel pot as he shooed the
children away from the tanks. A squall of machine gun fire
came from the windows above the street and caught him in the
neck, followed by rocket-propelled grenades against the tank
tracks. Morrison found cover behind a rubble pile, but many
marines did not. The sergeant spun in the street like a dancer
as more rounds tore his throat open until his head severed and
fell into a boiling puddle. The children were shot down in
turn, as were the wounded. When the tanks turned their tur-
rets to face the attack, the dead and dying were knocked from
the iron flanks, and not a corpsman was left alive. The men
screamed from the muddy street as the big guns reported without echo.

Morrison crawled back against the craggy wall. The cries
of the wounded were thin and lost and their bodies jumped and
turned from the machine gun bullets. He was with the remains
of his platoon, but he felt very alone, as if floating away from
the world of men. He closed his eyes, believing stillness would
never again befall this ground, then opened them. A wounded
marine without a shirt was crawling toward him, a boy not
much older than Morrison, his stomach opened and his innards glazed with mud. He moved his lips, speaking words
that went unheard, the rain dripping from his face as if he
were sweating out a nightmare. He put a finger to his head
like it was a pistol. Morrison shouldered his rifle and aimed
at his face. The wounded marine blinked his eyes, a smile

*forming from his mouth corners. Together, they found themselves in a pocket of calm while this boy with a face like his own begged him toward their strange communion. When Morrison fired, his head opened like a melon, the rivulet of blood drowning his twisted neck. Morrison waited to feel outrage at himself but nothing came. He then finished off all of the wounded marines with well-placed shots to their heads, the bullet sounds dull against the stone and flesh.*

Gus Dandallas ground a cigarette butt in an over-full ashtray and laughed smoke from his hairy nose. Morrison sat on a metal chair and faced this fat man. He had not taken off his field jacket. When the Greek leaned back in the swivel chair behind his desk, his stomach bulged and pushed against the buttons of a blue silk shirt smeared with cigarette ash. His face was like a rotten olive. Ashes also flecked the graying chest hair that snarled and half hid a ropy gold chain. Morrison laughed when he saw more ashes in the tiny hairs of the fat man's left ear.

There was a window in the office that looked down on a meat market stall where by day Gus Dandallas distributed whole frozen lambs to Greek and Arab butcher shops in the city. At night it became a card den, where waiters from the Greek restaurants along Halsted Street came to gamble away their tips. The dark-eyed men sat around folding tables covered with squares of green felt and drank Ouzo and strong coffee. They sorted their cards in stony silence, their ties pulled down, their shirts opened to the third button. The pots were filled with bills and watches and gold chains, rings with red gemstones from Greece, a few IOUs written on paper scraps. An old man in a black wool fishing cap made their coffee on a hot plate, his lips sunken into his mouth because he had no teeth.

Gus looked soft-eyed at Morrison, pursing his lips as if he were forming a sentence before speaking it. The stubble of his beard was black and gray, as were the hairs growing down from his nose.

The ex-cop is lost like the ex-priest, he said. I think I know this pretty well.

You know what I was, Morrison said. It wasn't a priest. Not by a fucking stretch.

No. But I think you are lost the same way. God does not want you and neither does the law. No more brotherhood for Danny Irish. That was gone forever the day they found cocaine in his piss.

I don't know what you're talking about, Morrison said.

You miss the badge like a priest misses the collar. I see it in your face. You are a sad man.

I don't know nothing about being a priest.

You can be like something without seeing it for yourself.

Morrison said nothing. The fat man puffed on a new cigarette, the smoke rising in clots. He scratched his stubbled cheek with two fingertips and smeared it with more ashes.

I am glad you have taken my offer seriously, Gus said. But I must know why you were so long in coming. It has been a year since you chose cocaine over your cop brothers. Or was it that cocaine chose you?

I don't know, Morrison said.

The Greek laughed at his laconic answers. He moved his lighter and package of cigarettes around the desktop as if he were playing chess.

I am owed lots of money by these waiters, he said. I do not expect to collect half of it. But this is not the point. A man in my position must be taken seriously. That is worth all of the money owed to me.

What's my cut? Morrison said.

Twenty percent of what you collect from them. These waiters must learn that they cannot gamble with promises.

Thirty or I'm leaving, Morrison said.

The Greek squinted from the smoke, then smiled a frown.

I won't make you piss in a cup, Danny Irish. Your cocaine is welcome here.

Morrison sat like a stone, smelling the frozen flesh of lambs. He put his hands in his pockets to conceal their twitching, but he knew he could not hide his eyes from looking hollow.

Thirty it is, Gus said. You will find these men have little but watches, the gold chains they bought from a nigger's pocket. I only want you to keep them playing and paying. Do not kill them.

I don't want none of your ghanies working with me.

They don't want to work with you. They still love life.

I just have my own ways, Morrison said.

You now have your collar back, the Greek said. You are whole again.

I was never broken.

The things we tell ourselves, the Greek said.

Morrison pushed back in his chair and uncrossed his arms, but he made no effort to stand.

The Halsted bus was awash in yellow light and maneuvered the wet street like a weird airship, passing the storefront resturants of Greek Town without making a stop. Morrison clapped his gloved hands to warm them and waited in an alley off Adams for the waiter. The early morning dark was cold and gusting wind. The waiter was nobody special, just a Greek with a gambling problem who loved the turn of the cards and thrill of not knowing what would happen next the way a john loves getting naked with a faceless whore. The transients from the New Jackson Hotel staggered across the street like unstrung marionettes, their arms wagging, their arthritic legs bent or bowed from falling down stoops and getting hit by taxicabs.

Morrison squatted down between two dumpsters, then filled his aluminum foil pipe with an opaque rock. He tilted his head back and fired it with a Zippo. He sucked, holding the narcotic mist in his lungs, and soon felt the long throb behind his eyes.

*The black kid stepped from behind a junked car where the alley dead-ended against a warehouse, waving for Morrison to cut his lights. Morrison sat in the squad with his partner Mateo and they glowed green from the dashlight. The black ranted, rolled his eyes, cursed these cops like a man beyond disgust, dressed in a Chicago Bulls sweatsuit, new Air Jordan basketball shoes. His head was shaved and glowing, his legs as long as streetlamp posts.*

*Mateo wiped the sweat off his forehead with a napkin he'd gotten with a pizza slice down on Taylor and Western. He was short with a power-lifter's build, an anvil with legs, a profane cop who liked blow jobs from streetwalkers the way Morrison liked the head rush of cocaine. He loved what he could make a whore do for twenty bucks. Morrison turned off the engine and unbuckled his pistol belt where he sat. The kid was scowl-faced, calling the two cops motherfuckers with his hands.*

*Look at this asshole, Mateo said. He thinks he's on his way to the Stadium to help beat the Knicks. Every goddamn moper on the street thinks he's Michael Jordan.*

*He thinks he owns me now, Morrison said. This fucking kid really thinks he does.*

*Jordan wouldn't give these niggers the stink off his shit. I bet he even fucks white broads on the side. A guy like him don't got to be a nigger no more.*

*I'm going to get this fucking kid, Morrison said.*

*Shit, Mateo said. I bet Jordan fucks some real class hookers. Five-grand-an-hour types. Hookers so good you'll never fuck a regular broad again. Well, Danny, let's do this.*

*Morrison rolled down the window when Mateo stepped from the squad car, the pizza sauce staining his body armor like an open wound. He held his baton while the kid eyed Morrison and spat a wad of bubble gum on the hood. Spit gleamed from his teeth and lips.*

*I thought I told you never to come here, the kid said. Only the niggers cop here, not the police. You'll shut me down the* rest of the night. I thought we had all this shit straight. Mateo, you tell that dumb Irish motherfucker that he's going to have to wait for his rock.

You're one sassy little nigger, Mateo said.

You're two junked-up cops. Morrison smokes more shit than a freaky bitch.

Mateo waited with his arms crossed on his chest. He looked up and down the alley. Morrison put on his gloves. Fucking pimp nigger, he thought.

The kid guffawed and laughed goddamns to himself, then dropped a paper bag on the asphalt and backed away. He sneered.

Mateo picked up the bag, still greasy from french fries. He took out crumpled bills and crack vials and examined them like specimens.

It's all there, bitch, the kid said. You're just in the wrong place.

I don't get you, Mateo said. Calling the man a bitch who could send you off to dick camp for five years.

How do you know I ain't got five FBI agents watching who could send you off to dick camp for a hundred?

Morrison stepped into the alley without his pistol or baton.

You going to teach this little nigger a lesson, Danny Irish? the kid said.

When Morrison tightened the velcro on his body armor, the smile melted from the kid's face as if he had no mouth at all. He tried running but Morrison caught him by the throat and squeezed until he went to his knees. The kid sucked for air, his eyes bulging. Morrison let go of his throat to let him think that this was only some muscle to raise the rent. The kid pulled bills from his pockets like lint. Mateo took the money, smiling wide and greedy, while Morrison kicked him in the face like he was being too slow with the payment.

You just got to say you need more, the kid said.

Morrison kicked his throat and sent him to the alley bricks vomiting blood. He curled like a worm, received more kicks all over his head and face, and made no sound. He rolled, then *lay motionless upon his chest. His fingers opened limply and the bills scattered from his hand like dead leaves in the wind. Mateo was happy and laughing and chased every one of them down. Morrison spat at the kid and called him to his feet for more, but he didn't come.*

The waiter walked from the kitchen door of the restaurant and shivered, his shadow cast vaguely against the warehouse wall. He was a small man in a big wool coat that held the snowflakes a moment before they melted. He looked back down the alley, over both shoulders, then walked with his head down against the wind, his face thin and polite. He turned west down Adams, heading toward the lights of a closed gas station, when an airplane broke the dark air beneath the clouds.

Morrison flicked his cigarette butt into the gutter flow and crossed the street after him. The headlights of cabs bore past in harsh shrouds. He wished that this made him feel alive again; he had even hoped for it.

The waiter wore dress shoes and took short steps in the snow. His pant legs were soaked. Morrison squared his shoulders and walked fast toward the waiter, then stepped into the small man's shadow.

Albert Sinadonis, Morrison said.

The man knew immediately what the smiling ex-cop wanted, and he ran with one hand pocketed, but slipped to his knees because of his soft-soled shoes. He broke his fall with the heel of his hand. The collar of his coat was upturned and half hid his head. Morrison grabbed the waiter's neck as if he were a dog and pulled him into an alley behind a snow-lined dumpster. The man was trying to take his hand from his pocket. Morrison lay him over some wet garbage bags and pulled the .38 from his pants. The man shuddered and looked away, crossing his hands in front of his face. He was older than Morrison thought, almost too old to stand this roughing.

You know why? Morrison said.

The waiter coughed and nodded, even pissed himself. The shadow of Morrison's hand holding the pistol fell perfectly across the man's stomach.

Five hundred will keep me off for five weeks, Morrison said. Two hundred for two weeks. Do you get how this will work?

He stared cruelly at the hacking man and aimed the pistol at his forehead. His pants were bunched about his knees; spews of mud clung to his hairy ankles. The El train sped brutally along the dripping tracks, the white lights drawing away into the night. The metal rush was loud enough to muffle a pistol shot and the waiter knew this because he dug through his pockets without watching himself and threw the crisp bills on the snow.

The young soldier sat in the curb and vomited beer between his legs, his eyes bulging as he spat the sourness from his mouth. Out in the street the rain streaked the windshields of Camaros and Trans Ams, just off the used car lots of Bragg Boulevard and over-full with crew-cut soldiers, and it smeared the neon signs of pawn shops and pool halls and beer bars across the blue gray night. The soldiers waited at a red light, gunning engines with rolled back miles, thrashing their shaved heads to loud rock music. Their pockets were hot with mid-month pay and the main gate of Fort Bragg was in their rearview mirrors, if only for a few hours. The boys in a pickup with Michigan tags threw beer bottles at the soldier in the curb, but most went long and splashed into the ditch water.

Wilder drove Thomas and Keller and Jack Tyne off post in his old Ford LTD. His time in the army was down to three days and a wake up. He held the wheel and rolled down the window, looking at the soldier sitting cross-legged and drunk in the curb, his blue jeans wet through from the gutter flow. Keller and Jack sat in the backseat and Keller combed his short hair against his dark reflection in the window. Thomas was quiet and leaned into the passenger door as if he would jump out and run when nobody was looking. Jack Tyne counted the beer bottles bobbing in the ditch water so he would not have to see Thomas, his blue eyes looking at him like they had some special bond because their fathers were killed in Vietnam. Jack hated him for doing it. Yesterday in the chow line, while soldiers smoked and joked and waited for cheeseburgers and chili-mac, the willowy soldier kept asking him about how his father came to him in dreams and if he spoke or was he just there like a shadow on a screen. I don't know, Thomas, he had said. I don't know what the hell you're talking about. Tonight they were bringing Wilder out for his last drunk over his own protests, and Jack figured if Thomas came and drank beer and screamed at the whores that Keller might forget his girl hands and slender hips that after two weeks were still drawing whistles in the latrine, the old jokes about soap on a rope.

Wilder jutted his small face out the window. The drunk soldier was awash in the diffuse glow of headlights. The raindrops ran down his neck.

You need to get someplace? Wilder said to him.

The soldier hugged his knees and then raised his wet eyes, red as if bloody, before vomiting again. He looked like any of them, blue jeans and a T-shirt, freckled cheeks with some acne, his hair so short it didn't have a color anymore. The cars honked at the red light for being too slow in turning.

Fuck this guy, Keller said. This dumb son of a bitch doesn't have any sense.

Get in, Airborne, Wilder said. You look like a goddamned wet dog.

The drunk soldier lay back in the roadside grass, his
pimpled face turning the rain as if it were pocked glass.

I hate to leave him, Wilder said.

Jack said nothing. He kept seeing Thomas' face after
the night they would come for him. His nose broken, his
cheekbones turned to powder. Jack understood they were
all waiting for Wilder's discharge on Monday morning because they knew he would tell the MPs everything out of
spite. A man with three days left in the army had no respect for barracks law. Wilder walked around the buffed
hallways and let the maniacs know that without saying a
word.

Keller shook a match cold when the traffic light turned
green. He was dressed collegiate: boat shoes and a wrinkled
oxford. He liked the soldiers to think he was a promising college wrestler but gave it all up to serve his country.

I'd hate to have to smell him, Keller said of the soldier in
the curb.

Shit, Wilder said, driving away. I'd hate to have to remember you after they let me out on Monday.

No way, nub, Keller said. I'm like herpes.

They drove out Bragg Boulevard, heading for the
Hiphugger, where topless girls sold one kind of beer and
charged a deposit on the plastic cups. The gutters ran
with brownish water and the lights of beer bars and clip
joints bled in the wet street. Slow-eyed whores called to them
from the sidewalks and Keller wiggled his tongue at them
all.

That drunk fucker reminded me of the Indians I'd see
when I went fishing in Canada, Keller said.

Indians? Wilder said.

Red niggers, we called them. We used to go fishing up
there in the summer. You'd see these Indians passed out
drunk along the bar ditches. Laid out like roadkill. The
bartenders would throw them out of the taverns for being

too drunk and they'd take to drinking Windex. You'd see the bottles strewn everywhere. People always think they're really into nature, but they don't give a shit.

When Thomas drew on his cigarette, he French-inhaled, the plume of smoke rising swiftly over his lip and into his nose. Jack shook his head.

It would be horrible to see Indians like that, Thomas said.

Is the fucking cherry talking to me? Keller said.

Shut your mouth or walk, Wilder said to Keller.

And let you motherfuckers ogle my ass? Keller said.

Jack watched Thomas fall silent as if he were a rock who had become a man and then turned back into a rock again. He settled back into the seat and looked out into the rain.

*I lost my way from the clinic in rainy Chicago and went searching for the expressway, down the endless streets of wet storefronts and trundling cement trucks. I had driven Gina up there for an abortion and we were far away from the brown river that flowed through our factory town, Watega, Illinois, where the sameness of life had a quiet brutality that killed most people without them knowing it. Gina sat in the car with her eyes cast down, her palm flat upon her stomach as if she could feel the absence. Her long brown hair fell across her cheeks and she made no effort to brush it out of her face. It looked like she saw the world from behind a waterfall. I went to touch her thigh and let her know that I was there, but she was so far away in her thoughts that I couldn't help wondering if she was making love to him. I left my hands on the wheel and looked for the expressway signs half hidden away in the clutter of the city.*

*Our mother gave me three hundred dollars in mostly tens and fives that morning. She was still in her housecoat and drew her cigarette in her dramatic way of tilting her head back and sucking smoke. You could look at her and see that she was once almost a beauty, but she had two kids and was widowed by a war before she was twenty; the man who was her ticket out of Watega was dead amidst rats the size of dogs.*

*What did he tell her it was going to be like that left her so bit-
ter when it didn't turn out? Would he have been any different
than the booze fat men in flannel shirts who people Watega
and go to high school football games so they can dream about
fucking the cheerleaders? She pushed the envelope across the
table as if I were being paid off, but the money was for the doctor who my mother was sure could abort Donny forever. The
fat man was gone with his acne scars and dog food smell; all
that remained of him were the burns his Winston Lights made
in the chair by the TV, and only his check and health insur-
ance benefits would be missed. My mother and I wanted to
think it was so easy. Get up there and come right back. That
was all she said. I had her brown eyes without any trace of my
father's deep blue, and right then I hated her for that most of
all.*

*I drove around the block, the wet streets already shining
light early in the afternoon. Gina looked at nothing but the
cigarette ash on the floormat. I wondered how it had started
with Donny, what line he had used to get her naked the first
time and the few times after that. I could not say I really noticed Gina or knew much about her; a fatherless son can never
finally get out of his own head because he spends his life looking for traces of the dead man deep within himself and finds
instead only a long black pause. We were never a family, and
the three years Donny was there went by the way you tumble
in a bad dream, the kind where you run fast but it's the world
that moves, not you. He came to fuck my mother and she had
him for his union benefits, even though factory unions have
lousy health plans. I thought of the day I would run him at
gunpoint from the bungalow that my father's death money had
bought. But there had been no explosive moment; he ignored
me instead of abusing me, perhaps not loving my mother
enough to see me as a threat. He went to work numb from Jim
Beam but never all the way drunk, only enough to ease the bit-
terness he felt about ending up fat and making dog food and
wanting to fuck his stepdaughter. My mother scratched for five
dollar bills working five nights a week in a restaurant run by*

*Greeks, a place where you order two eggs and get four.*

*We stopped at a red light by the clinic, a brick building without windows stuck between a video arcade and an Italian beef stand where people stood blurry behind the steamed windows. A man with a peg-leg sold newspapers in the intersection, his face like a cigarette butt. Down the alley, behind the clinic, were four dumpsters, overfilled with bagged trash and chained closed with padlocks. Half-hidden away in her hair, Gina looked at them as if counting the pigeons that whirred and pecked at the garbage bags. She had not taken her hand from her stomach.*

*Is that where it goes after they're done? she said.*

*I don't think so, I said. I didn't really know what they would do with a fetus.*

*Then where does it go? she said.*

*Not there, I told her. I hoped she would stay in her hair the whole way home.*

Wilder parked the car in the gravel lot of the Hiphugger where a big-legged whore was walking a drunk soldier off down a street of dark house trailers. The soldier had missing front teeth and a chin too small for his face and as he walked he palmed a handful of her backside. He walked bowlegged in cowboy boots. The whore was fat and grim and her hair, wet from the rain, stuck together in greasy strands. She kept moving his hand away so she could pull her panties out of her ass.

The rain danced on the metal gas tanks of three Harley-Davidsons parked along the curb and made the paintings of naked women and skulls shine in the moonlight. A yellow marquis on wheels, broken in places from thrown rocks, stood over a puddled pothole and blinked girls, girls, girls.

Now that's false advertising, Keller said.

Jack looked after the whore and the soldier, now just their dark silhouettes walking among the brown needles the rain knocked from the pine trees. Keller closed the door and flipped his cigarette butt at the sign, then watched how far it went over the puddle like he was playing a carnival game. Thomas stood and looked around, not knowing what to do with his hands, his thin body seeming to have been assembled from fallen sticks.

Quit menstruating, you pussy, Keller said to Wilder. You got two days left in the army and a good pair of boots to wear back home. That's a lot more than you came here with.

Wilder made a circling gesture with one finger at Keller over the car roof but stopped short of saying a word. He shook his head and pocketed his keys and sighed, as if to declare he could live without this going-away drunk.

The bar was built of cinder blocks with a flat tar paper roof that held a stand of rainwater. Jack could hear the drops boiling it. The building was windowless and had a vent and an exhaust fan spinning near the roof beside a broken TV antenna. A biker checked IDs at the door with a flashlight, his bloated stomach hanging below his black T-shirt and leather vest. He cocked his eyebrows and felt Thomas' cheeks for whiskers, then put his red face close to his. He talked from behind clenched teeth.

We used to have a faggot that reached down the front of your pants, he said to Thomas. He'd know if the ID was fake. He'd know it sure as shit.

Thomas stood twitching while the man finished with his cheek and handed him his ID.

What happened to him? Keller said.

The biker shined his flashlight in Keller's face. His forearms were hysterical with tattoos.

The faggot? he said.

Yessir.

He reached down a nigger's pants and we ain't seen him since, the biker said. True love, I'd guess.

Shit, Keller said.

You wanting his old job, Joe? the biker said.

I was just asking what happened, Keller said. Jack

watched him throw out his jaw in his way, getting half into a wrestling stance with his strong hands before him, fingers slightly opened. He could wrestle, really take people down.

I would have told you first off if I'd wanted you to know, the biker said. When a soldier boy asks, I know he's an asshole surfer big as life.

You calling me a faggot?

Jack pushed Keller through the door, his back muscles hard like frozen meat. They stumbled past another biker with long blond hair and the Sacred Heart of Jesus tattooed on his forearm, a black widow spider crawling up his neck. He stood with his arms folded across his chest in the way of fat men who want people to think them muscular.

You keep this soldier boy quiet, Joe, the man said to Jack. I see his future pretty damned clear and it ain't all that good.

The topless barmaids in their snagged g-strings pulled draughts of beer from behind three horseshoe bars. There were mirrors on the ceilings, mirrors on the walls strung around with blinking Christmas lights, an elfin redneck playing classic rock and roll on a turntable by the fire exit. The place was elbow-to-elbow with singing soldiers and many played air guitar and laughed with open mouths and waved their cigarettes like wands and bought tiny Korean whores grape Kool-Aid for three dollars a plastic cup. The girls wore their mascara to make their eyes seem round and told all the soldiers that their name was Kim but few ever asked.

They got some girls in this place, Keller said. I like to take my time in picking one out. The best ones come late.

At the rear of the premises, Jack Tyne could see the whores coming and going through the back door with their arms around staggering soldiers. The whores all wore garter belts that needed elastic and ragged satin teddies. The soldiers themselves wore a uniform even though they were out of uniform: cowboy boots, Levi's with a flare, black concert T-shirts from rock and roll bands they saw back in high school. Jack knew that only a year ago most of these paratroopers were sitting on the couch smoking dope and eating Fritos between their shifts of stocking shelves at K-Mart. Most of their recruiters never had to work very hard; they just sat behind their desks in some storefront on Main Street and waited for what the wind blew past. Jack also bet that half of them still had a prom picture tucked away beside the condom in their cheap PX wallets even though the girl was knocked up by some small-town loser who decided K-Mart was still better than jumping out of airplanes.

I was in here with Barclay and Winfield before they got out, Keller said. This whore was giving blow jobs under the table for ten bucks. Old Bark wanted to see what was going on so he pulled out his zippo and lit it. You know what happened?

I don't know, Jack said. He knew Keller was lying, but he went with it.

He caught the girl's bush on fire. The place smelled like broiled fish for a week.

They crossed the cement floor in the red bar light and coagulated smoke clouds and found space at the bar beside the stage where on the hour bored dancers shook fake breasts and cellulite backsides. They leaned into the bar like movie cowboys and Wilder and Thomas joined them and soon the new guy was set upon by a small whore with breasts no larger than fists. Her nipples were erect behind a beer-soaked camisole. Thomas was un-strung and searched the walls for something to see and seemed like a man about to fall backward and stay down. The whore clung to him and ground her slender hips into his groin and scratched his chest with fake finger-nails. Keller was yelling for the barmaid and waving a ten-dollar bill like a pom-pom.

Wilder spat tobacco juice into a drain on the floor.

Why did I let you talk me into bringing that new boy here? he said to Jack.

They'll ease off him now, Jack said.

Even Keller can see the whores make him nervous. That will give him all the evidence he needs. Shit, they make *me* nervous.

He needs to learn how to be one of them, Jack said.

The same way you did, Jack Tyne?

Jack said nothing. The whore was licking Thomas' neck and Thomas seemed deeply shamed.

You ain't got the sense God gave a tick, Wilder said.

He handed Jack his car keys.

It'll be yours in two days, anyway, Wilder said. You let Killer do his thing and come on back to the barracks.

Where you going? Jack said.

I'm taking Thomas the hell out of here in a taxi.

But this is for you, Jack said.

This ain't a memory I want to have.

Wilder looked at the whore sidled up against Thomas, then pointed to a bleary-eyed soldier across the room whose chin kept hitting his chest.

Now he's the one with the money, he said to her. Go talk to the man.

The whore ran over to him in her spiked heels and kissed his sweaty neck. The soldier let his face fall between her breasts. Wilder led Thomas back to the front door and the new guy walked with his eyes cast down. He straightened his shirt about his waist. He patted his jeans as if he were dusting himself off. Jack watched them leave past the bikers in the bar-back mirror and the one checking IDs blew Thomas a kiss.

Keller had four mugs of beer on the bar.

Them goddammed faggots, he said. I bet they even wake up when we're sleeping and take showers together.

That isn't true.

Fuck it. I ain't in the mood for a gook tonight. They always got this attitude and it's more like going to a doctor than getting laid. I really had my mind set on a black girl. I know just the place. Let's drink up.

A whore with saw-teeth came and took Jack's arm when he lifted his mug. The mascara on her eyelashes had clotted like roofing tar. He shook her away, even pushed her with the heel of his hand.

In the pine forest Jack and Keller glimpsed deer in the moonlight while they drove to the whorehouse, and in the moonlight the deer were as blurry as dreams and as fleeting. They leapt away from the headlights through the uniform trees and crossed the clay road by ones and bounded off into the darkness as if taking flight. The buck came last, moving slowly and with power, and shook woodvine from his points. Jack looked at the buck and the buck looked back at him before it disappeared into the thicket beyond the bar ditch. His eyes had glowed green yellow in the headlights and left trails when he turned. Jack felt something more than he could understand and thought about what it might be for a while after the buck was gone, but he let it go and watched the trees pass darker than the night.

Keller leaned over the steering wheel to see in the dark and the tree shadows fell across the road like rails gone awry. He pulled a pint of Jack Daniels from beneath the seat, shook it to check the level in the bottle, unscrewed the cap, drank, and passed it that way to Jack.

This yours or Wilder's? Jack said.

Payday whiskey is payday whiskey, Keller said.

But it isn't yours.

You don't really give a shit, Keller said.

Jack grinned and drank to the bottom, then pitched the empty bottle out the window and sat watching the moonlight streak the roadside puddles.

So you driving this piece of shit home in the summer? Keller said.

I'm driving it somewhere. I don't know if it's home. The

army sucks, but I still remember why I enlisted to leave Watega.

It isn't so bad being a soldier, Keller said. There's plenty of whiskey and hookers and enough money for both. Where else do you get paid extra to jump out of airplanes?

Keller was playing the cowboy. He used to slip lines from Clint Eastwood Westerns into conversations and pretend they were his own. He was like that.

You don't want to leave Fort Bragg, Jack said. Just go on and say it—I'm a lifer big as shit. One lazy ignorant fucker expecting retirement.

Where else do you get promoted for being a mean son of a bitch?

Say it, Keller—lifer.

Fuck you, Keller said. It beats the hell out of studying business administration at Rutgers. You have to listen to some jerk-off who hasn't done anything in his life but read and talk.

A dark overcast moved down from the north and closed shut half the sky. Jack wished there were more whiskey. It was better to be half tight when he got a hooker because later he could laugh it all off as a joke.

If I was back in college, Keller said, I'd be listening to some nineteen-year-old girl tell me how she's going to change the world by writing letters on behalf of death-row inmates. All so I could maybe finger her pussy. I couldn't take that shit after a while. A man shouldn't have to listen to it.

Jack shook a cigarette from the pack he kept in his pocket and put it in his mouth. He rolled up the window enough to light a match. He wished Keller would shut his mouth.

It's just easier with a whore, Keller said. You close your eyes and think about some other girl you wish you were screwing.

That isn't right at all.

They could give two shits. And don't go trying to kiss one.

They won't kiss? Jack said.

There's a few out here that will let you lick their necks, Keller said. But I don't miss kissing much. It's almost like having to talk to them. If a girl has nothing to say, a whore has even less.

The pine woods fell pitch black when the clouds drifted over the dome of the moon. They drove up the winding clay road another mile, the headlights burrowing through the humid dark, until they came upon a set of battered house trailers with white aluminum siding dirty from a hundred rainstorms. Keller took out the two twenties he would need from his wallet and hid it under the seat, putting the bills in his pocket. Jack did the same thing only slower, not as smoothly, and right then understood that Keller had always paid for sex and probably always would. His first time might have been out here in these trailers amid the locust strophe and the call of night birds.

The lamplight in the trailer windows was muffled by blankets for curtains. After the rain the night was hot and steamy, the air thick enough to put in a bag. A black girl came out of the trailer with a busted TV aerial and walked smiling toward the car with flip-flops popping off her heels. She moved unhurried across the wet clay on cat feet, her hands in the back pockets of cut-offs, as if a shadow creeping away from moving light. Keller smiled and licked his lips.

*Gina, you were so beautiful atop him, almost like you were his lover and you thought of nothing but giving to him, your eyes swimming in summer wind. I was more jealous than out-raged, more aroused than violent.*

The girl pointed at the headlight beams illuminating the corrugated trailers and sliced her finger across her throat. Keller grinned and winked at her, but both of his eyes closed. She sighed with an open mouth and shook her head.

You wanting to blind us? she said.

Keller cut the lights and shut down the car.

What? he said.

She rolled her eyes slowly. The salt taste of her skinny legs was on Jack's tongue and he felt dirty, a terrible sadness already within him like a lodger. *You were not raped, Gina, even if I wanted you to be and catch him holding you by the throat, muffling your screams with the palm of his hand.*

You both dating? the girl said. Or just one of you?

Lunch or dinner? Keller said.

Lunch don't fill nobody up, she said. But some men don't need that much.

A fat white girl was moving heavily across the tire ruts toward Jack's side of the car. One graceless, pathetic whore with gapped teeth and peroxide hair, her initials tattooed into her arm with a needle and india ink. She pulled her shorts from her crotch and walked funny because of it.

Keller's breath became an erratic pant when the black girl looked past him at Jack. He had his jaw out, as if jealous, ready to fight Jack for the whore's attention. She leaned into the car, her hard breasts pushed against her shirt.

I bet he's a real hungry man, she said of Jack. He knows how to eat it up.

The white whore knocked on the car roof where she slouched, stuffed into shorts and a halter like a filthy teddy bear. Flab hung off her back and thighs and she started stroking Jack's sweaty hair. He tensed and pulled away. When Keller saw this, he laughed, his mouth open, and got out of the car, almost leaving the keys in the ignition. Jack knew he didn't want to get stuck with the fat one. Keller and the black girl began walking up the cinder block steps into the trailer. Again he felt her hand, heavy, damp, and calloused upon his neck. The clouds swallowed the moon.

*Donny, you said, your lips curling your moaning, your hands flat on his chest. There you moved, Gina, your lips around his name.*

The whore opened the door, but Jack did not move. He closed his eyes when she peered at him in the dome light, a wet red face.

I could do something real nice right here, she said.

I'm fine.

I could get in there right next to you, she said. Ain't nobody going to see nothing.

*You go your way, Gina, I'll go mine. I can never let myself know the part of me that got hard watching you.*

Jack stepped from the car and closed the door and the dome light went dead.

I knew you were feeling a rise, the whore said.

They went into the trailer with the broken TV antenna, the cinder-block steps mortarless and just dropped on end before the door so they dug into the red mud beneath Jack's weight. Inside a young soldier and a fat black whore were joined on the bald carpet like mating toads. A bluish dark suffused the room. The soldier was a thin white boy who wore his baseball hat backward and knelt behind her, only the zipper of his pants undone. He held handfuls of her fleshy waist and thrust hard from his knees. Her eyes half closed and swimming, her lips pursed together. The thin mattress they used curled up against the wall. The soldier drooled and licked his lips and muttered curses, unaware of the intrusion, his teenage eyes gone feral for the moment. The girl seemed anywhere but there.

Jack Tyne's peroxide whore took a handful of shirt and pulled him through a curtain hanging in place of a doorway. The cloth smelled of cigarette smoke, cheap perfume, and must. She looked at him with slit eyes, less inviting than before, her belly the size of a man's. Jack looked away and stared at the water stains on the ceiling tiles, following them down the wall through their shadows like bruises.

It's forty bucks for a straight date, she said.

He held out the crumpled bills for her. The darkness hung like a great bulk.

I don't know if you're cop, she said. So drop them on the floor.

Jack did and listened to the soldier thrust against the

silent whore beyond the curtain. She counted the bills with her eyes, using a fast glance, then lit a cigarette and set it on a beer can used for an ashtray.

You know this is for one nut or until this cigarette burns? she said. You can't just fuck me for as long as you like.

I know that, he said.

She sat on the bed where the mussed sheets hung untucked over the mattress corners. One pillow was slumped against the wall without a case. Her belly rolled over her rutted thighs when she pulled off her shorts, blue scars like fishhooks on her hips. She went back on her elbows and spread her legs, her shorts dangling from a stubbled ankle. Jack Tyne's bowels churned as if from eating bad meat, and he looked away and sweat cold from his forehead while they finished in the next room. The faceless soldier wanted some of his money back because he thought he came too fast. He talked very loud out the door.

You need me to suck you hard, said the blonde.

No.

Then come on.

Jack walked out of the room through the curtain. The mattress was stained wet.

You ain't getting your money back, she said. You fucking faggot.

He looked both ways over his shoulders. The floor creaked when she stood to stuff herself back into her shorts. Jack put his hand over his mouth and fought back a sour heave.

Fucking yankee faggot, she said. Just come on back and try to get the money.

Keller sat giddy and squint-eyed in the car, singing along to radio songs, flushed from the closest thing to love he might ever know. He started the engine when Jack opened the door, then backed up fast and drove off throwing mud up from the back tires. Two crows circled the pine trees in the darkness.

Did she let you kiss her? Keller said.

I went to do it, but she turned her mouth away, Jack said. I told you.

You did.

Who did you think about when you were fucking her? Keller said.

Some girl I knew back home.

She wasn't much to look at, Keller said. But fucking is fucking. I didn't have to think about nobody. I liked mine but I might not see her again. They change whores out here a lot. They'll send these out in a week and let them fuck the marines in Jacksonville, then up to Norfolk for the sailors.

The trailers stood there, just silhouettes against the moonlight, when they rounded the curve at the end of the clay road and went on toward the highway.

Once black, never back, Keller said. Jack was silent. The pine shadows slurred on Keller's face.

You ever heard that said, Jacky?

Probably. I'm sure I have heard it before.

*I*n the cold rain Morrison drives his pickup truck down the streets of his youth; Thirty-fifth Street where the white bricks of Comisky Park fuse with the sheets of fog blowing east off the lake; the dinge of Halsted where the sons of Ireland spend their lives in nameless taverns and subsist on cold-cut sandwiches and draft beer. Along Emerald and Parnell are the two-flats and squat bungalows with gold stars in the picture windows for the dead of Vietnam. The stars stand for sandlot baseball players and golden gloves boxers and the crazy boys who killed cats for sport and the boys everybody thought were faggots. Old maids drink thick black tea and still talk of their brothers forty years dead on Okinawa; votive candles are still lit in their names each morning at seven o'clock mass, as if to keep the slaughtered from returning to seek vengeance against the living.

There are dark alleys where garbage cans roll from the wind and Morrison believes their wet bricks still harbor the last breaths of his brother who long ago taught him to use the alleys, know their dark. Morrison still sees his father stumbling drunk on cracked sidewalks, muttering half-words in Gaelic, so gaunt from drink that the lake wind thinks him a stick and blows him into parked cars. Morrison as a boy stands with his brother in the basement apartment and listens for the jangle of change in his trouser pockets while they wait for him to lie down on the couch and finally die.

1950 is the year of Morrison's birth. He comes at night in the damp basement of a two-flat while his brother watches with the gnome face of a child. His mother lies back flat on a mattress on the floor, her legs twisted in bloody sheets, biting his father's finger to the bone until he slaps her paling face and pries her teeth open with a butter knife. She has haunted blue eyes, hair blacker than night birds, a voice without volume. Outside, black sheets of rain blur the streetlights. She bleeds until she dies and then still bleeds, her dark hair unhinged and spread wet beneath her head as if a road puddle. The midwife cleans the mucus off him, and his brother is the first to hold him, wound in a quilt, while she washes her hands and shakes the water off her fingers because all of the towels are sponged with blood. His brother wears no pants and still pisses and shits where he stands, but in him is the vague memory of being mothered and this boy does have her blue eyes. Their father will forget her name and use black whores who loll about the back lots of the stockyards, but the boys remember as if it were a Station of the Cross. Philomena. Her name feels strange in their mouths.

The boys are skinny and unwashed and grow like alley dogs, often beaten by their father when he wakes them after his shift at the tavern. Many nights they smell other men's vomit on his clothes, see his eyes blackened by strangers' fists. They have dirty lips and runny noses and fevers; his brother's eyes are so runny and red that the priests at Saint Francis *think he is something from the outer dark. The boys learn to box at the CYO, instructed by the Emerald Society of the Chicago Police Department. The convent nuns feed them their suppers of soup and bread, find them shoes, coats against the November winds. His brother is a fine boy tenor and sings the laments of a country he has never seen in all of the taverns along Halsted. Hats are passed for pennies and nickels and the old men cry into schooners of beer and give folded dollars. In the sky the boys look for stars, but the city lights haze the darkness. Philomena, they say. Even his brother feels little except the name's strangeness in his mouth. He will pretend otherwise, even tell Danny that she is watching him from stars they have never seen.*

*At fourteen he is in a gang that has no name, wears no colors. The Irish cops love them and even recruit from their ranks. They fight blacks and Puerto Ricans along the banks of the Chicago River where derelicts watch from lean-tos of cardboard and cast-off tin. They hide baseball bats and chains and sharpened pipe lengths in the sewers and shoo away the rats after lifting the grates to collect their wares for battle. His brother is known for his violence, and his name haunts other neighborhoods. The Spanish call him loco; the blacks match him against four of their own. He slays boys with a baseball bat—a berserker in the city dark—outlined by the pale glow of streetlight. He swings first for their stomachs, then down upon their heads, smiling as they drool blood, drop their knives in submission, stagger backwards into chainlink fences. Many fall heavily and never move again. Danny watches his brother and learns, usually hidden away among garbage cans in the dark of gangways. The violence neither draws nor repulses him, though his brother is beautiful in a fight, worthy of an epic, his lean body, his well-honed punches and kicks. They no longer look for the stars, the hole in the sky that leads to heaven. Their mother's name now has the same significance as a street sign they walk past in the rain.*

*His brother fights a man much older than himself over an alley dice game. He blinds his eye with a bare fist, this fool* with a tic named John Doolin, his teeth always rattling between curses, saying everything two times: You know? You know? Doolin calls him a punky cocksucker from out of nowhere, then looks around for the others to laugh, but they are not laughing. Danny's brother wastes no time hitting him square in the jaw so that Doolin's head shakes as if it is an echo. The men let them fight in the headlights of a turquoise '60 Impala, as if they are warring cocks, even forgetting the action of the craps game and placing bets. Danny's brother moves inside and closes with three hard jabs to Doolin's right eye, the punches solid, successive. Doolin goes to his knees with his face in his hands, wailing. He will never again see a summer craps huddle with two eyes, nor the sweaty beer bottles, the fast-smoked cigarettes, the neighborhood girls dressed up like nightingales for the winners. But the young men do not care. He is a jerk-off, a silly-faced son of a bitch, a real fuckhead who picks fights with teenagers and loses.

Two weeks later Danny walks the back streets of his neighborhood where the Irish, lank, beer-gutted, stumble heavily from tavern doors with their hands over their mouths to puke on car hoods. He wears Levi's folded at the cuff, a T-shirt without sleeves, his hair shiny from Vaseline. He passes Noonan's Tap and inside a TV boxing match casts conflicting shadows across the faces of the drinkers at the bar. Johnny Doolin, wearing an eye patch, comes from a stool by the door and grabs Danny where he walks the sidewalk smelling the dead pig that wafts up in the wind from the stockyards. Doolin drags him by the neck into an alley and holds him against the wall by the throat, breathing sour beer breath into his face. The men inside laugh that Johnny has found one he can take. He pulls a .38 from his pants and shoves it into Danny's stomach and dry fires, laughing like the mad. Danny readies himself for death and spits into his face still swollen from the beating. He is pistol-whipped until he can think of nothing. Later that night, his brother's face will be riddled with .38 bullets and dumped in back of the yards among the polacks and bohunks, where little kids find him curled between garbage cans among the hog stench. *The kids startle the rats back into sewer grates. Danny does not know this for sure, but he imagines it this way.*

He takes beatings daily because many seek to kill his brother again though they would never fight him in life. His father feels no grief—only drinks—one afternoon becoming crazy from grain alcohol and kicking holes in the walls. He drinks from the bottle because not a glass remains unbroken. At night Danny roams the street like a tomcat, carrying a piece of sharpened pipe because he seeks to end the scourge upon him. He is not a big boy, but his muscles are lean, his hands quick. His delicate blue eyes draw compassion from old ladies and nuns, the neighborhood girls dream him their own, but of women he knows nothing and he thinks of them even less. He wanders barrios, the basketball courts outside housing projects, as if seeking ghosts. He watches derelicts gouging at each other's eyes with broken wine bottles on West Madison. He fights unknown youths with his hands, teeth, homemade saps, the sharpened pipe, boys whose smell of sweat, cilantro, and pork innards tells their stories, boys from neighborhoods and parents so much like his own that standing over them where they gasp in vacant lots, Danny sees his own death. He is not tough, but he is becoming that way.

Soon neighborhood boys are dying far away in towns whose names he cannot pronounce. An Khe, Ia Drang, Pleiku, Bien Hoa. The gold stars appear in picture windows. One night he walks toward the cool of Lake Michigan when John Doolin, gnashing together his teeth, jumps him in an alley behind the VFW local and shoots him in the thigh with a pistol. He is shot at again but missed. Pigeons jump from the power lines, taking to crazed flight. Doolin points to fire, showing his teeth, but the pistol clicks. Danny looks into his one eye and puts a homemade knife into his heart three times, then watches him die with the shank crooked in his chest. He leans against a garage door with blood running out of his pant leg. Two-flat windows go dark, curtains are pulled closed. He sits on the ground and waits for police sirens but none ever come.

*Three months later he boards an airplane at O'Hare with
many boys like him headed for the United States Marine
Corps Recruit Depot at San Diego. In the sky he looks for the
hole that leads to heaven but sees nothing except the rain
clouds fallen to storm.*

Morrison crouched between two parked cars southwest in
the city with the snow reeling before him in the wind.
Smoke curled into the starless sky from the bungalow
chimneys. He could see his ex-wife walking with a black
man through the snow squall, their laughter trailing off
when a vanload of tightly shouldered Mexicans drove by
with mariachi music playing so loud it set off car alarms.
The music faded away as the black opened her two-flat door
to the white-lit entryway. The black was big through the
shoulders and he moved in the swaggering way of a man
who wore very tight clothes. Her eyes were deep into his;
his mouth was open. They kissed for a long minute while
the man held the doorknob. Her hair was down over her
eyes in a way that Morrison had never known her to wear it.
Years ago it was always pulled tightly back in a bun because
he liked to watch her take it down and smell its sweet damp-
ness from having been wound after she washed it. She was
the plain-faced daughter of an Irish cop then, the neighborhood girl who spoke no words and sat on the rooftop with
him the night after he came home and listened to all he had
seen and felt. But her way of calming his nerves meant
nothing after a year. He began to feel things, yearn for the
whores of Asia who fucked him for small things of value,
giving their bodies as if they were not in them. He used to
like to pay his wife to have sex with him so he could pretend
she was a hooker. He made her refuse his kisses and remind
him that he only got one nut and another would cost. It was
the only way he could get hard. He left her years ago after
he sucked his service revolver and threatened suicide for a
reason he could not remember while she slid down the re-
frigerator door with bloody lips.

The black pushed her inside the doorway and she let herself fall against his thick chest. She smiled as if she were dancing and he bore the confidence of a man who knew he was going to get laid, even if he said the wrong thing three times in a row. Morrison took out his pistol and waited for the lights to come on in her apartment, but they never did. His breath drifted in the vague light when he stood between the cars. The snow slowly filled their footprints along the walk and up the stoop. He aimed the pistol at the dark windows and dreamed of shooting at himself.

*The sniper was anywhere on the third floor of the hotel on the day their divison commander claimed that Hue City was cleared of all NVA cadres. He took wild shots at the work details from graves registration where they lifted the bagged corpses into the canopied bed of an idling deuce-and-a-half. The men dropped the corpses when they ducked the fire and the driver rolled out of the door with a cigarette still in his mouth. The rounds chinked the deuce's hood, tore holes in the canvas canopy. Many of the zippers on the body bags were broken, and hands and heads and feet fell from the green plastic after being dropped. The faces of the corpses did not look dead in the rain the way they did in the sun.*

*Morrison sat inside the wall of a courtyard where he crawled to be clear of the sniper fire in the street. His knees and elbows were bloody from having crawled over burst concrete. His helmet was dented from a bullet. His eyes were red and swollen and the rain fell in them. He chewed a peppermint Chicklet while a .50 out in the street poured fire into all of the hotel windows. Half of his platoon was dead, but he didn't care because they had all hated him for being new.*

*The three VC suspects knelt without blindfolds and cast no shadows on the puddles. The tile roof of the villa had collapsed inside the walls, and an oak armoire leaned out of a window spilling a woman's lace underwear into the mud. The men were bound at their knees and their hands were tied behind their backs. The South Vietnamese officer paced before*

*them in a soaked khaki uniform and screamed his language
like a hysterical cat. The three men knelt quietly in the rain,
their oriental faces showing nothing, as if stones on necks.*

*The officer pistol-whipped a suspect, cleaving open his
head. Morrison lit a Camel. The man knelt in a puddle of water and wore no pants. Blood ran from his forehead and was
thinned by the rain. The other three knelt quietly. The officer
had laid the pistol barrel across the crown of the man's head
and grazed it with bullets. The VC was expressionless while
he lost consciousness and the rounds chinked against the wall.
The officer and his men laughed like boys. Morrison smoked
and watched the VC slump forward as if drunk. He was half
awed by what a body could take before quitting. The VC was
not yet dead when the officer started in with the next man.*

Morrison walked off up the street made narrow by snow-
plows, then over to the Cermak Avenue truck lots where
the ruptured night watchman stood silently in the yellow
window square of the guardhouse by a chainlink fence.
The filthy gutter snow came up over Morrison's ankles
and the razor wire atop the fence dripped wet upon his
head. *What a pistol could do to a nigger's face without even
killing him.* He fought the urge to remember his ex-wife's
name; then he couldn't remember much more about her
than that. In the guardhouse the night watchman
scratched his eyebrows at the troubled stranger's passing
and held his side as if to keep his guts from spilling out.
Morrison was red-eyed. He knew he looked bad, perhaps
crazed, like a man on the verge of drowning.

The kids by the corner liquor store were skinny blacks
with hard eyes, and their shadows fell long across the foot-
printed slush. The windows were dim-lit and cluttered
with placards for Hennesey and King Cobra, and small
bullet holes pimpled the glass door. The kids were alive in
talk where they had posted themselves outside the liquor
store to shoulder-tap a drunk to buy them booze.

Morrison drank half a pint of J&B in three swallows,

then crossed the street toward them. He staggered from
the delayed hit of the Scotch and tried to hold his eyes
straight. Plywood sheets covered the holes in the sidewalk.
He stood on the boards and eyed these kids until they fell
silent. The tallest among them squinted his narrow eyes
and peered out from a hooded leather jacket. In his ears
were two gold hoops.

Evening Officer, he said.

Morrison blinked hard and the three kids reeled like
shadows from a strobe.

You wanting your dick sucked, Officer? the kids said.

The others covered their mouths and their bodies
shook with laughter as if they were coming apart. Morrison walked closer, the sky and sidewalk closing in upon
him like a vise.

We ain't sucking no cop dicks, the kid said. His face
seemed molded from frozen slag. He pulled his hood
down. Cornrowed braids ran across the crown of his head.

Morrison felt for his .38.

Get the fuck against the wall, he said. All of you assholes.

The cheap policeman wants to hack us for nothing, the
kid said.

I told you cocksuckers.

Look at this drunk bitch.

Get against the wall.

The policeman can't even talk his shit.

The kid charged him while the Scotch smeared Morrison's sight and turned the night molten. His eyes were
bleared from cheap booze, as if he had already been
drunk twice that day. Morrison was fumbling for his pistol when the kid tackled him. They went into the curb
snow together. Morrison was back flat on the ice and he
smelled the cold sweat of him, the stale beer on his
breath. The kid was hitting him in the head, clean jabs
with big fists. Morrison rolled onto his side into a riot of
kicks and ugly laughter. The kid stood and fetched him a

boot heel to his face. Morrison tasted blood. The snow gathered on his face while he lay motionless and felt fast hands frisk him for his wallet. For some reason they left the pistol. The flurries fell from the blue gray night like pieces of broken cloud.

J ack Tyne and Keller lay back flat on their bunks on the night before their discharge when Thomas was to be beaten bloody for the faggot rumor. The window was open to the hot night of winds, filled with silent heat lightning, the thin wires close and scarring the dark sky. In the hallway, Cross, the gimp-legged extra-duty, kept losing control of the floor buffer that went sliding over the dribbled floor wax and banged into the room doors. Pecha, the doper from second squad who had made private first class three times that year, yelled out through his locked door that Cross sucked monkey dick and ate whore pussy and would even pay to give the fat black ladies who worked at the PX rim jobs even though they had more facial hair than Specialist John Anthony

Dominic Donatelli from South Philadelphia, the soldier who First Sergeant made shave twice a day, his face under a perpetual shadow. Cross just let the buffer slam into Pecha's door until the doper only yelled motherfucker and cocksucker and son of a bitch and then figured silence would beget silence and shut his mouth.

Jack looked over at Keller, who feigned sleep, then at their duffel bags packed and slumped against the wall. Keller with the Tom Cruise eyes and the smile that matched. Keller the talentless kid who talked fast, who had not reenlisted but probably would tomorrow in a final sentimental outburst. Keller the loudmouth and failed jock with whom Jack had been joined for four long years and who after tomorrow Jack wouldn't walk across the street to watch slash his wrists. In twelve hours it was all done; Jack would never have to look at Keller's game-show-host grin and see the man who might save his life, grease the gook or Ivan or spic who had his AK-47 pointed at his head. For four years, Jack stayed friends with every soldier because he never knew when they would trade in floor wax and paintbrushes for fragmentation grenades and live rounds, going from janitor to killer in a matter of hours.

Keller sat up in bed when Cross finished with the hallway and stowed the buffer in the platoon closet. He wore a black sweatshirt with a hood even in the heat and walked to the door, dropping two bars of soap into a sock before knotting it, then waited for Cross and his bad leg to hobble downstairs and smoke cigarettes with the duty sergeant and cuss his condition. Jack Tyne rolled to his side, the sheet twisting in his legs, while Keller unlocked the door and stepped into the shiny hallway.

That evening Jack and Keller had moved through the chow line for the last time, the cooks slapping at the hands of grabby soldiers with spatulas and serving spoons. *Keep your dickskinners to yourselves, Airborne.* Their white plates steamed with succotash and breaded veal patties and rehydrated mashed potatoes. Fredericks waited in the short-order line, impatient as a dog, hoping out loud that the cooks would not run out of onion rings before his turn came to order a chili dog, the meal he'd been eating twice daily since he came to the battalion. The hungry soldiers cussed the cooks who moved as sleepily as cats and smiled while they served from vats of rice, salted only from the sweat running down their tattooed forearms. Jack and Keller fell in with their trays and headed for the massive coffee urn with five spigots that served what the top sergeants called lifer juice, holy water, joe.

*Gilligan was looking for extra motor pool guards last Saturday afternoon, Keller told Jack. He had the master keys from the first sergeant's office because none of the new guys answered when he knocked the first time. You know how it goes: when the CQ comes looking for guards, all the barracks rats climb out of windows and hide in wall lockers. Remember when I caught Fredericks with his idiot grin hanging from the window ledge like he was doing pull-ups, the fist-fucker so hungover he was drooling. Gilligan starts unlocking doors to find nothing but the curtains blowing in open windows. He hears the loud fucking hells when the new guys hit the grass outside the second-floor windows. Nobody was home except your buddy Thomas. The faggot was lying naked on his bunk and jacking his queer dick to magazines full of naked guys in leather jackets and cop hats. Thomas was really working his elbow. Gilligan just told him how he better drop his cock and find his socks and be downstairs ready to walk the post in five minutes.*

When their hard bootfalls sounded down the hallway, Jack turned twice in his bunk. They were coming for Thomas, and Jack figured there were five of them, their faces like raw bacon, their shaved heads hidden away in black sweatshirt hoods. Two to hold him and three to beat him; that was how it always went. They had the first sergeant's master keys and the keys jangled together, loud in the quiet barracks, before Thomas's door opened and closed quickly. It would all be done very fast, humane as far as a beating went, lasting only a minute. Jack stared at his lumped shadow against the cinder-block wall and saw Thomas gagged with balled skivvies and his wet eyes blindfolded by an ace bandage wrapped around his face, then left on his back and duct-taped to the wooden bunk so his delicate body could accept the blows of Ivory soap knotted into the toes of green army socks, his face convulsing like an epileptic in seizure. Jack covered his ears with both hands and rolled over, burying his face, open-eyed, into the pillow until he saw spots.

*My mother stood finishing a cigarette when Gina and I came back from the abortion clinic in Chicago. She wore a pink housecoat that she hadn't been out of all day; her hair was matted from sleeping. There was a pillow and blanket on the green sofa, a glass of jug wine on the coffee table. The house was dark except for the blue TV light. Gina walked right past our mother, her legs so skinny that the insides of her thighs never touched, moving off down the hallway through the drifting smoke to her bedroom as if a figure receding into the fog. She seemed little more than a shadow, the consistency of gusted wind, so cut loose from the world now that nothing could touch her. Where did she think they put the dead fetuses? Where did she think they went?*

*I watched my mother snuff the cigarette in an ashtray on the coffee table as if she wanted to sear the glass. I unbuttoned my wet mackinaw while she kept grounding out the snuffed butt.*

*You're dripping all over the goddamn place, she said.*

*She came toward me with a dishrag bunched in her hand. The TV light shifted colors, turning the cigarette smoke blue and white and red. She knelt and wiped my dripping off the linoleum, picking up a dead leaf that had fallen off my boot. I wanted to ask her if she could wipe the day off of me, this moment in my life that was becoming beyond my power to forget. She wiped and wiped, this woman who cannot stand finger-*

prints on walls, throw pillows out of place. Outside, the tree branches, black with rain, bent in the wind. My mother rose with the rag balled in her fist, herself three heads shorter than me. The smoke and jug wine had reddened her eyes.

You got a cigarette? she said.

I gave her a Marlboro from my coat pocket and lit it with a damp match. She inhaled and blew the smoke out from her crinkled face, as if disgusted.

I don't know how you can smoke these shitting things, she said.

You don't got to smoke them, I said.

They're too goddamn strong.

She smoked and looked out the window with trembling lips. The wind blew rain off the tree branches. She wrapped her arms around her breasts. I could have said anything to her but I did not. I wanted her to shiver by the drafty window, her eyes dripping like the trees.

Billy Mahone snuck through Gina's windows for three nights a couple of months ago, she said. I heard him. He was the little son of a bitch that got her pregnant.

Her bleary eyes watched me from their reflection in the window. The rain was slanting through the dark image of her face. What a life of losing will do to the soul, I thought.

You need to get that little bastard, Jacky, she said. You are her brother and she has no father.

My mother pressed her face against the window, smogging the glass with breath, moving closer and closer as if to join with her reflection. She didn't look at me when I walked out the front door with the wind blowing rain and dead leaves back into the house.

I went down the street beneath the curled branches of willow trees and then cut through a back lot to the next street as the rain became a thick mist. I wanted to believe her because a boy as pretty as Billy Mahone could have done things to somebody's sister. He was nineteen with this long, soft girl hair—the kind of kid who never wanted high school to end because he somehow knew those were the last days he could dream himself a rock and roll star. He worked at the lumberyard loading two-by-fours and sheets of plywood in the back of contractors' pickups while the old men pointed at his hair, asking him if he squatted when he peed. I would see him driving around Watega in the white Camaro he restored in the high school auto shop, more body putty than metal, always with a vain teenage girl who played with her hair. He wore sunglasses while he cruised around Friday nights singing along with his loud stereo, hamming as if he'd written the rock songs himself. I never liked him anyway.

It was raining again and I could smell the wet street and the car exhaust lingering in the rain. I ducked in between two bungalows, squat and brick, and lit a cigarette out of the wind. Bird nests were falling from the thin oaks. I walked to the alley and took a metal lid off a garbage can. For a minute I was a kid again, the lid my shield, a length of broomstick I found in a trash heap my sword. I swung at my shadow cast vaguely against a garage door as if I were a knight. But the smoke from the cigarette in my mouth burned my eyes, and the afternoon whistles of Roper Stove and General Foods called the second shift to their lines. All of it brought me back to why I was in the alley behind Euclid Street. I spat the butt into a puddle and headed for Billy Mahone's house. The rain was flooding back-yards and wet dogs waited silently on porches, their food dishes filling with water. I swung the lid at the drops the way a fighter shadowboxes.

I wanted to hurt him because there was a softness to his eyes that life had not touched. I hated him for driving around Watega in his white Camaro, singing radio songs with pretty girls who liked the wind blowing back their hair, while I walked the alleys knowing that the truth of life was a gut-shot marine staring off the way dead men stare. How could he drive and drink beer and park on the river bluffs to fuck underage girls in his backseat? I didn't even know him, but I loathed the asshole for being stupid enough to enjoy his youth and drive that Camaro just to drive. He had to see that men were little better than dogs. I wanted him to at least know that.

*It was an hour past twilight when the Camaro with dual exhaust pipes pulled into the gravel space behind his parents' bungalow. The back door light blurred in the black sheets of rain. I was soaked from squatting behind a woodpile where the rain disintegrated piles of dog shit. My thoughts took strange turns until I stopped having them, my mind almost like a piece of night. His windows were tinted and with the hard rain there was no way that he could see me. He sat for a while inside the car until he was finished listening to a radio song. I had become hollow, made of a straw, a good soldier. You can convince yourself of anything, even your own lies, and there really isn't much to it.*

*I let Billy step from the car and close the door before I fell upon him without noise. I watched my shadow go with me. His long hair was wound inside a baseball cap and my first swing with the garbage can lid knocked it from his head into a puddle. I swung at his pretty face the way I had practiced, down on the head, up against the jaw. Billy's hair was in his eyes, wet from the rain and nose blood. He went down to his knees and fell three times upon his hands. His eyes were closed. He did not know who was beating him.*

*Sit dog, I told him. I said sit.*

*He crawled through the rain while I hammered his lean body, my fingers numb from holding the cold metal without gloves. The alley gravel stained his jeans gray. He coughed and spat and I laughed like a pervert. Then he collapsed on his side, the raindrops running through his blood-smeared face like sweat. I felt nothing. I sent the garbage can lid spinning off through the darkness and ran for home the way I had come.*

In the morning an MP lieutenant named Stangel and the company commander entered the barracks room with the anxious glances of hungry men who must finish a job before eating. Keller called attention with a booming voice, and he and Jack locked their heels on the shiny floor tiles. Jack and Keller wore their dress green uniforms with their trousers bloused into spit-shined jump boots. Captain

Merkel, the company commander, crossed his arms before his chest so that his West Point ring would glint in the sunlight slanting down through the window glass. He was a peacetime officer, promoted solely because he could run marathons and the army liked men who were good runners. He checked the ribbons on Jack's and Keller's uniforms for regulation display, as if he were an upperclassman back at West Point ready to haze plebes, douse them with chickenshit. His eyes were drawn asshole-mean on his face. The MP lieutenant had a thin face and sighed his boredom after talking about the beating of Private Andrew Thomas to sixty soldiers, all of whom claimed to know nothing about it. He left Jack and Keller at attention and looked at them with neither suspicion nor humor.

Private Thomas, the MP said, was found wandering Ardennes Street last night with busted cheekbones and a barracks bag full of civilian clothes. I want to know who threw him the blanket party.

Is that what happened, sir? Keller said.

The MP lieutenant eyed the floor as if he were looking for someplace to spit.

How did I know that was going to be your answer? he said. I bet you were asleep too, just dreaming of fucking lollipops?

Yes, sir, Keller said. I was asleep.

The MP looked at Jack while the company commander was searching the room for potential demerits the way he had learned at West Point.

What time was Corporal Keller in his bunk? he said.

In the waxed floor, Jack saw himself hanging upside down beneath Keller. His stomach sank. He couldn't swallow. He knew it was all an act for himself because he had decided already to lie.

2200 hours, sir, he said.

The MP sighed heavily and rolled his eyes. The company commander was looking off down the hallway where the rest of Bravo Company waited in their rooms to be questioned. His hands were on his hips, the West Point ring forever prominent. There was little else about Captain Merkel to notice and perhaps he even knew it.

Are you aware of any homosexual activity regarding Private Andrew Thomas? the MP asked Jack.

No, sir, Jack said.

It's the cliché, right Airborne? the MP said. The bad fall. The slip on soap.

I don't know, sir.

Of course not, Airborne. You are not paid to know, you are paid to do. Sometimes you all just do too fucking well. I have nothing else.

The company commander was already out in the hallway when the MP officer turned and walked through the door. The MP almost half gave a shit, Jack thought. Not all the way, but enough. Keller called attention while Jack looked out the window. Alpha Company was marching in off the parade field after a long run, and the soldiers were exhausted and dehydrated-looking, their T-shirts darkened from sweat. They sang in loud cadences and their arms swung in formation like dirty dishrags. *If I die on the Russian front, bury me with a Russian cunt.* When the officer's bootsteps faded down the hallway, they sat on their stockaded bunks and lit cigarettes, using the lid from a can of Kiwi shoe polish for an ashtray.

Fucking hell all right, Keller said.

He smiled like a game show host and kicked his duffel bags stacked at the foot of his bunk. Jack glimpsed him and nodded and watched the smoke diffuse into the thronged sunlight. Keller squinted from the smoke in his eyes and motioned up and down the hallway with his cigarette.

We always kept a clean room, Jacky, he said. Cleaner than most of these assholes ever did. Merkel couldn't find shit. Fucking officer prick.

Yes, Jack said. We did.

They can't say nothing about us when we're gone.

When is your flight home? Jack said.

Keller sat and held the Kiwi lid under his cigarette. He went to answer, but his eyes welled with tears, as if he understood that he was very lost.

They'll be hard-pressed to find one dustball in this room, Keller said. We are squared the fuck away. Aren't we, Jacky?

We were.

Two dirtbags will move in, you know that, Keller said. Two limp-dick cherry motherfuckers.

They might.

Two big pieces of shit.

The cigarette gave Jack a headache but he smoked it for something to do with his hands.

You know, Keller said. I'm not all the way right with leaving today.

Jack tapped his ash and let it fall on the floor. He didn't care anymore. Keller was letting some of the tears fall, his face taking on a red sheen. He forced a smile, but his lips trembled from the corners of his mouth.

I am a good soldier, he said.

They sat. Neither spoke. Soon their last cigarette together was smoked. Jack snuffed the butt in the lid and stood to wipe the gray ash off his trouser thighs. Keller's hands shook as he lit another cigarette, end to end with the smoked one, watching Jack sling his duffel bag over his shoulder. He was waiting for Jack to say something and Jack knew it.

How many jumps did we make together, Jacky? Keller said.

Eighty-six, not counting the five in jump school.

Remember when we did the twelve-mile ruck march in two hours and five minutes? We set the fucking battalion record that day. Remember the sergeant-major and the old man came into the chow hall and had lunch right with us.

I do.

But none of it means shit after today, Keller said.

It will all depend on who's listening.

It's over, Jacky. Isn't it?

Yes.

Even if I stuck around the company for three more years it wouldn't be the same company. Everybody's discharged or transferred. They say First Sergeant is even set to retire. But out there, nobody will even give a shit.

You're right, Jack said.

He watched Keller smoke like he needed nicotine to breathe.

Why did you guys do that to Thomas? Jack said.

I don't know. Maybe for the old company.

Have a good trip, Killer.

Jack nodded at Keller and left the room before he had to shake his hand. His reflection followed him all the way down the hallway to the staircase and he felt much the same way about looking at it that he had about shaking Keller's hand.

**D**ogs troubled Morrison's dreams and he could not sleep an hour. He hallucinated that packs of frothy-mouthed curs with missing eyes ran through the city blocks after him. Last night he woke and heard five barking in the alley off Monroe and Sagamon. His rented room was lightless and barnlike and he lay on his bare mattress waiting for death by mauling. But the alley went quiet. He knew there had been neither dogs nor sounds. The room was not yet paled with morning gray. He listened to himself breathe, afraid to close his eyes because he knew what form his dreaming would take.

When he was a marine in Vietnam, the platoon had an Indian radioman from New Mexico who claimed without boasting that his father was the highest Acoma holy man in their pueblo. His face was flat, as if made without cheekbones, and it already bore wrinkles from hard sunlight at twenty-one. He was a tireless walker, drank little water, and ate grasshoppers like a cat. His father sent him off to Vietnam because the old man felt the wandering souls of all Native men who died so far away from their ancestors. The dead must be danced for. This was his only purpose in Vietnam, and he volunteered to carry the radio so he would not have to kill NVA or VC. He wore things in a small leather bag around his neck and even the two Lakota men from the Black Hills of South Dakota thought him crazy for his chanting and joined the other marines in calling him Chief or Tonto.

After the Battle of Hue, Morrison's platoon was clearing the tunnels that the North Vietnamese had used to infiltrate the city by sending in stray dogs to trip the booby traps. The marines won the trust of the dogs with C-Ration ham and laughed as they sent them to their death. They laid odds on the minutes it would take for a dog to set off a rigged grenade, fall into a pungi-pit, get bit by a coral snake tied to the tunnel roof. Some of the dogs took a half hour to die, especially when impaled by the pungi sticks, wailing the long minutes away. This made the Acoma man very sad, more reflective than outraged. He told the marines that the dog was a gift of friendship and love from the Everywhere Spirit and that they were making war upon His love. One day, he said, they would all have their night dreams ravaged by dogs with cold, feral eyes who fell upon them in soundless packs. Morrison laughed with the others.

Morrison lay on his back listening to his heart surge beneath his breastbone. Last week he had come awake and seen the dogs for the first time. He was wound in a dirty sheet and crashed from cocaine. Their black forms ran ahead of their darker shadows, their yellow teeth glowed in the night heat, dripping froth. The room spun, its space filled with the smell of hot, wet dogs that bit and tore at his legs, his sweaty face. He felt deep wounds forming and his hands came away wet when he touched his face, but he saw no blood. He did not want to die mauled by rabid dogs, but on his feet: a marine, a cop. For a time he slept with a pistol taped to his hand until one night he heard the hysterical barking and came awake squeezing the trigger without aiming. The muzzle flashed. He jerked the trigger until the hammer clicked against the empty cylinder. The cracked plaster above the window was gored by bullet holes, the broken glass shined streetlight from the warped floorboards. He got up and staggered to the window, his body awash in a chemical sweat, the pistol smoking in his limp hand. He looked down at the street where a fat whore was stabbing at the door of a boarded storefront with a knife, screaming at the hot desolation.

He sat awake for a long time, terrified to lie back down on the bed. Once he thought he heard a bark beyond the street and the El tracks, but he did not know for sure. A dairy truck trundled down Monroe, setting off a car alarm, and he thought he heard barking in that. He stared at the broken window and waited for the gray dawn, placing the pistol barrel against his throbbing skull from many different angles.

By night Morrison worked the streets and saw no natural light. He traded his boots for basketball shoes and blackened the laces with shoe polish so his feet would fall soundlessly as he stalked the slow-eyed filchers down the dark hallways of transient hotels, cleaving open their doors with a fireman's axe when his knocks went unanswered. They might beat the Greek, but they would never beat him. He wore the colors of night, loose jeans and T-shirts, and he faded into the midnight air of Greek Town along Halsted Street, where every morning the waiters hosed wino piss off the sidewalks in front of their restaurants. The broken gamblers, the fat men made orgasmic by risk, countered

Morrison by sleeping fully clothed beside windows open to fire escapes. The ex-cop bribed security guards and late-night desk attendants to knock for him while he climbed the fire escapes, meeting the filchers high above the street with his .38 stretched an arm's length before him. They begged for their lives like bad actors and Morrison secretly hoped that one would put him to rest.

With a pocketful of money and watches and rings of little value, Morrison walked toward the Greek's stall in Fulton Market to give him his share. He took a dark-bricked alley north of Madison Street where bums of all races, crazed from drinking canned heat, waited outside a men's shelter for a baloney sandwich and an apple. Their eyes were red, their lips black from filth. Hot wind gusted from the south and dry thunder rolled along the edges of Chicago without the promise of rain. The sky was gauzy. Emaciated whores who tricked for ten bucks called out to him from warehouse doorways. He entertained himself with dreams of potential ambushes, men with pump shot-guns or automatic pistols in both hands killing him be-neath the dark girders of the Lake Street El tracks. He imagined the faceless men drinking up his money in some tavern without a name while he drifted upward through the night clouds to the hole in the sky that led to heaven. He could hear the El cars passing behind him like the sound of some phantom disaster. *Mercy is what I showed them with their guts staining the rubble after the tank knocked them off its flanks to kill more gooks. Mercy is what I ask of them now.*

Two black kids watched him come up Morgan Street toward the railroad tracks. They sat doubled-up on a junked bicycle, the banana seat stripped of foam down to a long piece of rickety metal. There was a snarl of weeds be-side the tracks where the Mexicans had parked a car to sit on the hood and laugh while they drank canned beer and pissed into the flurry of light from the passing commuter trains. Neither black kid wore a shirt or had laces in his tennis shoes. Their lank bodies already bore fine muscle tone. The smallest one cried and his skinny friend shook his head in disgust.

Shut your mouth, Kenjuan, the friend said. Danny Irish is going to hear you.

Kenjuan sucked snot back into his head and then stared at the potholed street.

You're walking if you don't shut your mouth, the friend said. Then Danny Irish is going to make you pay to walk his street.

Morrison stood before the two kids and smoked. A small wind gusted across the heaped waste of garbage bags and broken bricks. Kenjuan raised his bleary eyes to it. The friend strained his long legs to keep their weight balanced on the bicycle.

I told him that you're going to get him, the friend said to Morrison. And he don't got no money to pay you.

Go easy on your little brother, Morrison said.

He ain't my brother. He just stay with us.

You still got to go easy.

I didn't hit him. But I could. I just can't stand his crying.

Tears warped Kenjuan's sight. Morrison knew the kid was seeing the world as if through bad glass. He remembered himself behind his brother on a bicycle they stole from the Italian kids at the Notre Dame Academy, sitting outside Comiskey Park to beg the drunks for dimes after a night game.

Why's he crying? Morrison said.

Them spics over there got a dog that's dying, the friend said. It got hit by a car or something and it's just laying there in them weeds. Kenjuan thinks its his old dog and I keep telling him that he never had no dog.

Morrison reached into his pocket and handed the friend a twenty-dollar bill.

You split it with him or I'll get you, he said.

Honest, the friend said. It's mine.

It's his and yours.

That's what I mean.

The kids rode off on bald bicycle tires, the toes of Kenjuan's shoes dragging through the gravel and the potholes of dirt. Morrison wiped his brow and looked after them. Their bodies disappeared in slow tandem until he heard only the slipping of the bicycle chain. He headed for the tracks.

The Mexicans were small men and their beer cans dripped cold water from the ice buckets onto their shoes. After the commuter trains passed, grimy paper blew along the tracks as if mocking the motion of tumbleweeds. The car they sat on was blue with a green fender and red crepe paper was taped over the brake lights. Two men were pissing on empty beer cans without watching themselves, their necks lax from drink. The dog was in the weeds between the shadow of the car and the raised crossing gate. It lay curled on cigarette butts and shredded newsprint with mangled haunches black from blood. It was glassy-eyed, pestered by flies, soundless as if resigned to suffer before dying. Morrison could see that the dog was watching the ways of these drunken men.

A stout Mexican swallowed his beer and staggered up to his feet from where he sat on the car hood. Morrison knew him as Anselmo; he worked as a butcher of goats for Ayala Meats on the market street. The cuffs of his faded jeans were stained with blood and fat, the slime from tripe and brains. He walked closer to the dog. The other men drank and fast-talked Spanish and paid Morrison no mind at all.

Hey, Danny Morrison, Anselmo said. Some motherfucker hurt my sweet bitch real bad. I wait to see if she live or she die. I drink so much because I love her.

The dog looked at Morrison without raising its head. Flies snarled in its mangy ears and crawled across its eyeballs. He knew the dog was female because he could see teats had begun to form and her stomach was heavy and bulged between her hinds.

How long has this dog been here like this? Morrison said.

Anselmo was laughing.

My bitch? he said. My bitch suffered a long time. My bitch made no sound and suffered the whole night. All her life she's been with me; she's in love. But this is all she had to look forward to. Mourned only by the nigger children.

Morrison and the dog met eyes. Eyes in which the darkness was absolute. He pulled his .38 out of his belt and put two rounds, point blank, into her head. The carcass jumped and spun; the dust rose like waves. Anselmo laughed and swayed backwards, breaking the silence caused by the shooting. Morrison shoved his pistol back into his belt and turned away with a terrible sadness. He did not look at the dog anymore. Some men laughed while others tilted their heads back so that the beer would pour faster down their throats.

Anselmo wiped sweat off his unshaven cheek.

I told her to go away from me, he said. I told her many times, but my bitch loved me too much. I was not a good man for her.

Morrison took a deep breath as if he were diving under water. Anselmo grinned and pulled a wet beer from the ice bucket. The ex-cop reached for it.

Come on, Danny Morrison, he said. Now we have the wake.

t was hot and windy and not yet dawn the morning of Jack Tyne's return to Watega County, Illinois. He drove the Ford LTD he had bought off Wilder through the fields at the east end of the county. The yellowed cornstalks glowed from the moon, and the lightning shifted their shadows between the furrows. The dust marred the windshield like rain, and he smelled the drought upon the country; soon he hacked up gouts of brown phlegm from the dust. He rolled up the windows and drove through the two limestone columns that marked the entrance to Saint Joseph's Cemetery. The country was wrecked, the corn dead before the stalks were knee high.

The wrought-iron gate was tied back among the tall weeds. The hot wind sucked the wilted leaves of the oak trees that lined the gravel drive into the cemetery. He parked the car and got out, the army already seeming a lifetime ago although he had been discharged for less than twenty-four hours. Keller, Wilder, and even Thomas were as good as dead to him. He walked up the narrow lane among the tiny stones and crabgrass snarls where small American flags, dry-rotten and left over from Memorial Day, marked the grave sites of dead veterans. There were pieces of plastic flowers and styrofoam vases strewn across the grass burned to dirt, and he kicked them away like cans.

The first leaks of gray dawn crept over the fields as he came upon a simple VA headstone flat in the earth. He wiped the dust from his eyes and came slowly forward. The grass crunched under his boots. In his blue jeans he stood in the pale light. Two crows flew cawing off to the fields to gnaw the broken cornstalks. Along the rowed graves were VA headstones of forebears he did not know, all of their names engraved in flat, bronze sheets. The oldest among them was his grandfather's uncle who died in 1899 while fighting in Cuba. He looked at his father's name and stared at the letters until the words seemed like some forgotten language. *John L. Tyne. 1946-1968. United States Marine Corps. Republic of South Vietnam.* His eyes bleared with tears the way he knew they would, and he turned toward the hot morning wind to dry them, but they never dried. He sat on his father's name and hugged his knees.

*I once walked with my grandfather through this cemetery with my child's hand lost in his. He squeezed it without knowing, the rough callouses on his palm scratching my fingers. My grandfather was a plumber and had a strong grip from a lifetime of holding pipe wrenches. He was a surly man with gentle polack eyes, blue in the way of rivers from cheap landscape paintings. He limped when he walked fast from the shrapnel off a Japanese grenade that broke his femur bone on Saipan. He called the scar his zipper because it ran all around his right thigh, and he would tell me that he took off his leg at night like he did his pants.*

*The cemetery grass was wet from a night of soft rain, and he drug me along the rowed stones. I stumbled three steps behind him in his long-flung shadow. Our footfalls were mute in the solitary yard. He stopped at many graves and leaned forward to read the names from his boyhood and the faraway places of their deaths etched into granite or bronze. Tunisia, New Georgia, France, Sicily, Okinawa. The names themselves reading like a roster at Ellis Island. Gotto, Pajack, Konicki, Armenise, DiBrita, Siezmenko. His eyes always became wet, though tears never fell. In the autumn he would bend down to wipe dead leaves off the stones, but of the men below he never said a word.*

*We crossed the gravel lane and walked up into the cemetery past the concrete crucifixion and past the pauper's markers with their small memorials. Bundles of goldenrod. Empty pint bottles of Early Times. A small ceramic Virgin. The green fields stretched beyond the two whitewashed crypts where the parish priests lay, this land more flat than a librarian's chest, the old man would say, the wind tender in the cornstalk tassels. My father's grave site was where it always was, just beyond an oak tree but not close enough to fall under the shadows of its branches. Neither one of us looked. We knew it was there.*

*The old man walked me to the oak tree and then stopped with his cap in his hand. The cigar butt he chewed stained his lower lip with a thin band of tobacco juice. He would limp no further because he never did. The oak tree could have been a rimrock mountain with its peak lost to the clouds. Once I saw him look toward the grave site and kiss the wind as if it were his dead son's cheek. But that morning he only stared off at the fields in his way, then cursed silently in the Polish he spoke as a boy. He let my hand fall and then put on his cap and leaned against the oak as if to steady himself against a windy squall, but the wind was faint. The leaf shadows half hid away the deep seams of his face. He put his arm around my bony shoulder and pulled me against his bad leg as if he were holding his dead son again.*

*He was life to me after so much killing, the old man said. My baby son came that first spring of peace like the blossoms on the apple trees. I loved him. Your grandmother would laugh at the way I smiled changing his diapers or bathing him or humming some made-up song when he cried in the night. I could look into his small eyes and see none of it, those days when I was using a flame-thrower to burn the nips out of caves when they refused to surrender. Smelling it all and tasting it for days and becoming so used to it that when I breathed clean air, I liked to have choked. But it was more. I liked burning those sons of bitches. He made me forget that side of myself.*

*My grandfather fell silent and looked out at the cemetery, digging his boot heels into the grass.*

*You know he ain't even down there, the old man said. The Marine Corps sent back his casket empty. There was nothing left of him to bury.*

*We stood by the tree while the white sun burned off the clouds. I waited for him to tell me something about my father that I did not know, but he was silent and staring off miles beyond anything. The country filled with goldenrod and the shadow of the stones became more definite in the harsh light. There were small flags that the arthritic men from the VFW put over the graves of veterans every Memorial Day; many had been knocked down by the rain, but a few stood. I already had the habit of the old man not to look and see if my father's flag was there. We walked down the gravel lane the way we had come, only now the old man did not hold my hand, nor would he ever hold it again.*

Jack was run through with bird shadows while the sun burned his face. An old Ford pickup loaded with rakes and shovels came dragging dust along the gravel lane, passing freshly dug graves and a canopy set up against the sun to shade a hundred folding chairs. The parapets of dirt that would refill the hole were already blanched the dry, brown color of the wind. The truck backfired after shutting off.

Two old men in green work uniforms got out into the dust wake with lunch pails.

One of the gravekeepers sat down slowly beneath a young hickory, using the low-hanging branches to help himself down. He ate a sandwich and rubbed his knees, looking out at the ruined fields in the unfazed way of old men who are sure they have seen worse. The other man was more spry, and he walked smiling toward Jack, his shoes scratching the crabgrass and the weeds. His skin was red and doughy from the sun. There were blue veins like electrical wires on the backs of his hands. Jack looked up when the man's shadow covered his own.

Excuse me, son, the old man said.

Jack smelled the coffee on his breath when he spoke. The black paint from the cemetery gate flecked his green shirt.

It ain't a good thing to tell a visitor to get, the man said. But I have to do it. The funeral party will be along inside the hour. The flowers are right behind us. They got to time this right so they don't wilt.

When Jack stood, his legs cramped from having been asleep. The old man looked at him cautiously, maybe thinking him a doped-up kid, perhaps crazy because Jack could tell by the tightness of his throat that he'd been talking to himself. The other gravekeeper whistled while he arranged the yard tools in the pickup bed. His knees had a permanent bend.

It ain't like I'm shooing you away, the old man said. But I got to.

Who died? Jack said.

The gravekeeper bent a smile when Jack spoke in a normal voice.

The old priest, he said. Father Stremkowski. Half the polacks in the county will turn up.

He scratched his unshaven cheeks and inspected Jack's face, his red eyes, his GI haircut.

You'd think something really happens when you bury

a priest. Nothing does. Everybody dies the same. But the people got to come to see if anything gets transfigured.

Jack pointed down at his father's grave.

Did you dig this hole? he said.

The old man chuckled lightly through his nose.

Me and Howard dug them all before we got too old, he said. Every one since 1946. We ain't had any other job except for being sailors during the war.

Did you dig this one?

I'm sure I did. I just don't remember the details.

The old man looked down at the bronze sheet and his lips moved as he read the lettering. His face was like a crushed brown bag.

Yessir, he said. I buried all of those boys. Every one. Even Howard's nephew Pete Grezlak.

Jack's eyes burned. He knew these old men would rather call their wife a whore than say the word Vietnam.

He your relation? the old man said.

My father.

I knew your Grandpa Walt from the old days. Your Uncle Eddy, too. Ed never came back from France but I guess you know that. He was a neat kid. He would have been someone to know. Wars have always been hard on Watega. I'm sorry about Walt's passing, but I laughed something loose when I heard Walter Tyne wanted to be cremated and have his ashes dumped in the Watega River—

So his enemies wouldn't have the chance to piss on his grave.

That's right, young man. You either loved Walt or you didn't. And there was a lot who didn't.

Thank you, sir.

Come on back around three, the old man said. The show will be over by then. Everybody will be disappointed that no angels swooped down for the old father. I never had use for the son of a bitch other than him signing my paychecks. He said some things about my daughter after her divorce. You can't forget people's circumstances. You can never do that.

94

Jack walked off and got in Wilder's car and for a long second thought of the fat whore with peroxide hair standing outside the window.

In two miles' driving, Jack crossed the Watega River at Waldron Bridge and took Route 113 along the banks of dried and cracked mud. The shallow brown water was still as rocks and showed sandbars and beached deadheads. Water snakes coursed through the sickly color that the sunlight cast upon the river. He drove east toward town, past boarded stove factories and foundries where weeds snarled through the cracks in the parking lot and the chainlink fences were spotted with white birdshit.

Old men sat on buckets and fished uselessly from the Court Street Bridge, their shadows upon the sidewalk like bodies fallen over. He went past Aldens and Carsons department stores with no fineries on view behind the dusty windows, only lease placards offering so many square feet, then past the bronze Union soldier who stood watch on the courthouse lawn while hamburger bags crept in the gutters from the hot wind. The parking meters were gone like the town, this commercial street reduced to vacant storefronts and unnamed taverns and a currency exchange where the welfare poor stood in a long line while their spastic children gyrated and wrestled on the sidewalks.

He drove the curbless streets of his boyhood, the neighborhoods gone with the factories, past battered blue and white bungalows built of cinder blocks where TV antennas rose from rooftops patched with tar. He parked the car before a railroad viaduct under the watchful eye of a fat woman who sat on her front steps in a floral nightgown and drank RC Cola. Across the tracks were the basketball courts of Tubman Park where he'd wander on summer nights, a pale boy the blacks thought suicidal, unfazed by the taunts of peckerwood, grayass, honkey, as if a deaf man. He stood outside the fenced courts and watched the midnight games and waited to buy a nickel bag of pot while the blacks passed sweaty malt liquor bottles and smoked thin joints that smelled of mint, toking them off their lips with fast draws. *This shit is way too motherfucking harsh.* One night he smoked a sherm stick with a mixed kid named Marshaun, blue-eyed with hair straight like Jack's, banished to watch the games through the fence where shirtless men threw elbows and gouged eyes to move the ball between the baskets. The two of them sat spaced on the curb, watching the workmen at General Foods shovel grain from the boxcars into vats raised on forklifts. He told Marshaun the story of his life, the sad details about how he liked watching his stepfather fuck his sister, until he found that he had not said a word.

His uncle's house was whiter on the east side than the other three walls, as if the painters stopped midway through the job. The gravel driveway went through a gateless chainlink fence and was littered with beer tabs and cigarette butts. Jack put his hands on the fence and pulled them away, burning.

Uncle Walt sat in the garage on a metal cooler with an open beer beside his thick-soled brogans. His skinned hands held a cutting torch, and he halved an I-beam with its thin, blue flame. The tanned skin of his forearms was so burned with the blisters of his welder's trade that he appeared a collage of many different races. The hot orange filings fell to the cement floor and burned to black.

Jack's bootfalls in the gravel were lost to the sound of the flame cutting heavy metal. He walked up to his uncle and kicked his boot. Walt looked up in welder's goggles, then twisted the torch knob slowly so that the blue flame went orange from the loss of acetylene and the pure oxygen fire chuffed black smoke. He turned off the oxygen after he lit a cigarette with its flame.

Hey Uncle Walt, Jack said. You know anything about this poor slob whose wife made him get a vasectomy and then threw his ass out of the house he built for her?

You home legal? Walt said.

Can you still get a hard-on?

If you weren't my brother's son—

You'd throw me out of your truck at Tubman Park and yell nigger.

Hell, Walt said. Them guys would just turn you loose on account of your mouth and then come after me for making them listen.

They laughed and smiled at each other like old comrades. Jack loved his uncle, his father's lone brother who went off to Vietnam in late 1969 knowing that there was nothing to win. Walt was not his grandfather's favorite, but he was the brother who came home to show the old man his Silver Star in its patent leather box. The old man only looked at the medal with his sad eyes and asked Walt when he wanted to start working; they were putting in the plumbing on three new houses on the North Side over by Saint Rose's and he could take him on as a laborer. Walt called him a son of a bitch, left town the same day he came home, and stayed gone for six years. Where he spent those years changed according to how much Jack Daniels he drank back with his Bud draughts. Sometimes Mexico. Sometimes California. There was even talk of three years in Europe. He couldn't keep his own lies straight in the end. He finally came back and started working for the old man.

Walt grinned wider at Jack and scratched his beard. The Marine Corps globe and anchor tattooed on his left forearm, once fine with detail, had become a lump of splotched green. He stood up on his haunches enough to open the cooler he sat on and handed Jack a cold beer.

You look good, Jack said.

Better than last year, Walt said. Veronica had me going to AA meetings. I'll tell you, Jacky, there ain't no future in listening to a bunch of sober drunks high on caffeine. There were grown men crying and hugging each other right in front of women. I ain't ever seen so many cake-eaters in one place. I thought the world was coming to a fucking end. She had me reading a book about a god-damned seagull that thought like a person. All them drunks read it and thought it was the Bible. We just got to use our imaginations to make this shit better, Veronica tells me. That's what this book is about. Now how in the hell is that different than boozing?

You might live ten years longer.

It ain't worth the struggle. Ten more years of crapping into a colostomy bag if you give up bourbon? But hell, using your imagination to make this shit better? Where's anybody seen this shit better enough to know how it should be? I kept putting that question to them.

What did they say? Jack said.

Not a goddamned thing.

Jack saw that labor and booze had done a job on his uncle's eyes. Their soft blue was encased in rounds of wrinkles that told of early mornings in taverns where he drank and ran his lines of shit on divorced women dreaming of tenderness. Walt drug his cigarette and shook his head like a man who was tired of hearing his own mouth move but knew it was the only act he had.

I checked myself into detox up at Hines VA last year, Walt said. You know, for Veronica and the kids. I guess you didn't know.

No, Jack said.

It wasn't bad at all. I was in a room with four other vets, all former marines. A lot of smoking and joking, you know. There was this pretty little girl up there training to be a shrink. She's asking me what I thought it was that got me to this end, that all I had to do was go back to the last good time and start over. I was stepping over dead gooks along the DMZ when she was in the third grade and she's sitting there telling me that my problem was that I use 'alcohol to medicate the effects of past trauma.' All I could think about was her squirming when I ate her pussy and the ways I'd use my tongue. It probably ain't been visited by three dicks.

I'm glad this drought hasn't wasted everything, Jack said.

Here's to a new generation of veterans, Walt said. May

it be a damned sight luckier than the last.

They clicked beer cans and Walt stared at his boot toes. He then drank up, mocking a smile.

I saw your mother, Walt said. Saw your sister too. I guess you know Gina's getting married next month. She told me who it was, but I can't remember. Your ma's still married to that farmer from Saint Marie. He must have a few bucks. She was driving this big yellow Lincoln. I wanted to ask her if she had Elvis in the back.

I haven't gotten a letter in two years.

You write any? Walt said. I know I gave up after you didn't come home when the old man died.

I'm here to see you, then I'm gone up the road.

The road's a bunch of shit, Jack. Runs in a big fucking circle. There's nothing but assholes on it.

Jack was silent and turned away. Sunlight showed white against the cinder block walls like the mark of some coming spirit. Walt took out two more beers. His eyes had turned red and glassed over. He held out a dripping can for Jack.

No thanks, Jack said. I'm still working on this one.

He reached the beer closer to Jack.

Go on, he said.

I can't drink them like that, Jack said.

Maybe not.

No, Jack said. I can't.

Walt lit a cigarette and blew smoke in between swigs of his fresh beer.

If I had a nickel for every beer tab in my life, he said. Funny thing is, I just like getting mucked-up. Anyway, I thought I'd tell you I saw them.

And I guess I'll tell you that I don't give a shit. I haven't even met that farmer from Saint Marie. All I know is that if he believes her bullshit, he really isn't worth knowing. What do you think?

Your mother is still your mother.

She moved on the same way Aunt Veronica did.

It ain't about moving on, Walt said. A woman really ain't much different than a man. They hate being alone the same as we do and they'll stick with whoever is around until they find somebody better. But people really don't move anywhere in this world but sideways.

I don't mind being alone.

That's because you ain't never been together.

Jack lit a cigarette and smoked it.

My mom never loved him, he said. I figure she was knocked up twice before she even knew it. Then he got killed in Vietnam.

Walt drew his eyes. He was becoming sentimental and pathetic in the way of a real drunk.

What the hell are you talking about? he said. You don't even remember him and her.

She never said his name. I remember her begging us to call Donny dad. There were all those other assholes that she was fucking in between.

Who told you this bullshit about her not loving my brother.

You did when you were drunk. Even before the old man died.

You didn't see her cry.

Okay, Jack said. She loved him and hasn't been able to live right without him. None of us have.

There's a lot I could tell you, Walt said, but I ain't. All I'm saying is that you go pissing things away, Jacky, they don't ever come back. You got to forgive.

You know what the hell I saw. Go on, tell me what it was.

Walt nodded and took a long drink from his beer and then cooled his wrinkled forehead with it. He pinched the ember from his cigarette and flicked the butt out the garage door. The ember was dead ash within a second.

The navy was actually wanting me to learn how to fix radios, Walt said. Back in 1968, that was a lucky break for a high school dropout. It could have transferred easy into

TV repair and I wouldn't be no welder with scarred arms. Knowing how to fix TVs is like owning a bar. Good times or bad times, people are always going to watch TV and drink. But I joined the marines just like my big brother did, thinking I'd find the gook that killed Johnny and send the motherfucker's scalp back to the old man. Maybe even do him so his gook family in the North got an empty casket sent back. But I had the aptitude to learn electronics. I wouldn't have had to go to Vietnam at all.

Walt paused, but not to let Jack speak.

Navy enlistments were at a premium back then too. In 1968, they were sending all the niggers, spics, and dumbass white boys to the army and marine corps and sticking them in infantry units. All of them went to Vietnam. The big nothings of the whole fucking United States over there killing gooks wholesale. Shit, if you had the aptitude to do anything, even count blankets or drive a goddamned truck, you weren't going to Vietnam. But the old man had a way of making it known that he'd of rather had me die for my country than Johnny. Funny thing was, Johnny didn't have the aptitude to fix radios.

I can't see that being true about the old man, Jack said.

That son of a bitch didn't want to teach me to be a plumber, Walt said, even if I was the only one who could learn. He would hardly let me touch his tools. He stopped seeing me when that casket come home empty. He was like some old man in a movie who ain't got nothing at the end of his life. He died thinking about it.

I always wondered what the hell Johnny did that was so special, Walt said. He knocked your mother up twice before she was nineteen. He could have gotten out of the draft, but he joined the marine corps like he was running off with the circus. I think he just played along with the old man's shit about being a plumber and burying your money in the backyard. The old man thought I'd send my inheritance right up my nose, and you know what, I did, right down to the last twenty-dollar bill. But I went off looking for Johnny's ghost in Vietnam. I didn't find it. I came back a ghost myself and the old man went right on looking through me.

Jack's eyes were wet and he looked at Walt as if through fogged glass. His uncle nodded and scratched his beard, then rose and walked out of the garage and down the gravel driveway. Jack went to the door. In the hard sunlight, his uncle staggered along the curbless street and toward the edge of the neighborhood where the withered fields spread for miles. He did not call for him.

That night Jack went after Donny. He found his address in the phone book in a booth outside the bowling alley where teenage girls sat on parked cars and smoked cigarettes and returned the catcalls from passing pickup trucks like hookers. They were chubby girls with red faces and big asses crammed into tight jeans, and some mocked fellatio on their pop bottles while cackling at truckloads of dull-eyed country boys cruising the curbless streets of Watega for the night. Jack sneered at them when he pulled out of the parking lot and headed for Liberty Gardens Trailer Park. One gave him the finger. Another patted her bloated backside as if for him to kiss it. He hated them back with his soldier's eyes. He still didn't know what he would do when he saw Donny.

He drove up the gravel lane of the trailer park, past a trailer heaved in half by a fallen hackberry as if a beer can crushed by a boot heel. The tree was enormous and charred black from a lightning strike. The mangled trailer was rowed with the other house trailers along the rutted drive like so many cars abandoned in a blizzard. Junked bicycles and cast-off mattresses and engine parts were strewn about, forming the yards into a single trash heap.

The ruts turned into a dirt road as he drove out to the edge of the cornfield and the dwarfed stalks glowed from the moon. He headed for an old barn beyond the field

where he drank beer as a teenager and lay on the hood of
Tommy Ruell's Firebird staring up at the sky frantic with
stars, dreaming of escape from the open spaces and
smokestacks while the other boys sat around the fire and
played drinking games with lukewarm Budweiser and de-
clared that when they graduated high school, they were
going to do nothing but get stoned. *Why do you want to join
the army, Tyne? You can't get high in the army. You can't roll
up a hooter and let Pink Floyd set you to sailing. You'll miss a
big party.* Jack was sure they were all working day labor on
construction sites now for cash under the table, waking up
every morning to call some cheap contractor and see if he
needed any footings dug for five bucks an hour. He always
hated them for thinking that they could party in life without having a thing to celebrate.

He parked the car and stepped out into an old firepit
filled with burnt beer cans and broken wine bottles. The
winds did not come again after the last big gust of dust and
corn chaff. The night was still. He opened the trunk and
took out an axe handle he'd stolen from his uncle's garage,
then shoved his K-Bar knife from the army through his
belt near the small of his back. *Not to kill him, but to knock
him down and leave a scar on his face so that every fucking
day he'll remember that I could have cut his throat and left
him to bleed in the hot dark. And that I might even come back
and scar his other cheek whenever I feel like it.* Jack swung
the axe handle and listened to it break air. The winds
mounted and rose steadily from the horizon, sucking gently among the shriveled leaves of the hedgerow between
the road and the paintless barn, perhaps even sounding
like rain. He headed back toward the trailers to look for
number sixteen. The mailboxes stood along the rutted
drive like teeth in an idiot's head. *It ain't nothing but a big
world of shit.*

The trailer where Donny lived was the last one before
the cornfields started and behind it the weedy lot ran up
against a dry creekbed. The windows had screens that

were ripped and stitched with thread. There was a car without an engine and tires propped up on cinder blocks at the end of the drive, and it was white from birdshit. The other trailers were dark.

Jack stood in the ruts listening to the distant whistle from General Foods call the midnight shift to the pack lines. The time was close, fifteen minutes, maybe twenty if Donny stopped at the J&L for a cold six-pack of Strohs Light and a bag of barbecue potato chips. Fat fuckers and their light beer, Jack thought. There were withered leaves on the drive from the hedgetrees off in the fields, and the dust was blowing across the leaves like water over rocks, gusting in waves through the darkness enough to haze the interstate lights two miles away. He glowed from the light of a thousand stars. He found a rusted toolshed between the carport and the trailer and went inside to hide where the air was still hot from the day.

He had smoked three cigarettes when Donny's pickup pulled into the drive. He snuffed his last one, then stepped back into the darkness, away from the headlights. Sweat ran into his eyes. He brought the axe handle up from its position straight along his leg and held it like a bat, moving to the front of the shed after Donny cut the lights. But Jack saw him before he struck. He was very fat and moved as if the weight bore down and afflicted his knees. He wore the same clothes he always wore to work the lines at General Foods, blue jeans and a faded T-shirt, forever stained red from the processing dye they used to color the dog food. Jack saw his face even if he really could not, the acne scars pocking his cheeks, his nose crooked from being broken, the thin red hair that seemed transplanted from some animal. Jack stayed inside the outer darkness of the shed. He could not move. Donny fell into a horrible fit of coughing from the dust, and the flesh around his waist bulged and rippled. The bagged six-pack fell out of his hand. He hacked for a long minute, doubled-over with his hands in front of his mouth, his shadow a stain upon the dirt. Jack Tyne slunk back into the shadows and quietly laid the axe handle against the shed wall. *If I was him, I would have fucked her too.*

The window of Morrison's whore was three stories above the alley bricks, a dusty screen in a six-flat. He dug in his pockets for a cigarette and looked up one last time because this was the night he planned to die. She was not watching after him, the blue-eyed black girl with skin like yellow daisies, the swan among so many pigeons who timed his love by burning cigarettes in a sooted ashtray, her small apartment a collage of diaper boxes and empty baby formula cans and potato chip bags and crushed pop cans. The price was forty dollars a cigarette for all the love he could get before the filter burned black smoke. There was always the sound of her boyfriend watching TV in the room behind the closed door, the stirs of her infant in a crib made from a box and a pink blanket. She kept him hard with her left hand and lit another cigarette with her right while he dug through his jeans rolled down to his thighs for the extra bills. He liked to kiss her shoulder and touch her face and nuzzle gently against the underside of her breasts. One time he thought he felt her moan, breath fast. He had memories of the Vietnamese girls in the brothels of Da Nang with their blue-eyed children sleeping on pallets beside the cot of their trade, the coolness of Morrison's metal dog tags between their chests while the kid coughed and whined.

Death would come tonight in a bar on Grand Avenue where fat Jesus Pagan ran cockfights for the Puerto Ricans and dogfights for the blacks in the dirt-floored basement that smelled of sweat, gin, and blood. There was a pit dug into the earth with a chicken-wire fence and in it the animals would war unto death beneath the naked lightbulbs. Morrison and Mateo used to gamble there amid the straw fedoras and gutter Spanish and pints of Bacardi 151 chased back with the deep draw from a Have a Tampa cigar. The roosters with long feathers gored at each other's eyes with their beaks and left flecks of blood in the raked dirt. Morrison, all blank-eyed from crack and Scotch, felt the gouges of lethal pecks as if he were the weaker bird, half terrified but very jealous. Mateo just threw his money down, his floral shirt open, cold beer bottles weighting down his pockets. *I love this shit, Morrison. I just motherfucking love it.* He planned to walk in after the fights when the house had the sweaty bills in the metal box, draw his .38, and shake the place down with the cocky swagger of a drunk cop. He'd wave the gun without aiming it, calling them cocksuckers, low-lifes, degenerate spic motherfuckers. Fat Jesus and his guys would just laugh and shoot him, hairy-gutted men with crucifixes tattooed on the whole of their backs, tigers on their forearms. If he was lucky, four automatic pistols would be firing into him at once, the bullets twirling his body as if he were a dancer, his last breaths the stale air laced with rooster shit and dog blood and the booze sweat of drunk gamblers.

He walked up an alley off Grand Avenue where in the garbage from a liquor store a man lay with his clothes stained from vomit and urine. His pale face was contorted from drink. Drool ran down the stubble of his cheeks. His shoes were gone and the arches of his feet were dark with blood. The shipping boxes for King Cobra malt liquor overflowed from the dumpster and set all around him like he was the victim of an avalanche. Morrison walked right past him. *If I could only pull on myself, it would all be done.*

The bar was the bottom floor of a brick two-flat and the windows were open without screens. Morrison crossed the alley and walked up into the gangway between the two garages, his shadow falling on the layers of spray-painted graffiti. The used car lot beside the bar had ten cars with their monthly payments soaped into the windshields, shiny but spent cars that people bought for their paint jobs. Morrison smoked in the heat and watched the back door of the bar where an old black man left cursing with a dead dog wrapped loosely in a blood wet blanket. His coal face was dark against the lighter night, his silk shirt open and wrung wet. The hairless hind slipped from the cover, the flesh gnawed red by the victor's yellow teeth. The man stomped like a child who had lost a game and dropped the dead dog in a dumpster full of beer cans, then called it a motherfucker. He walked off on crooked legs and fanned himself with a soaked fedora, sipping from a pint bottle he'd taken out of his back pocket. *Punkass dog cost me five hundred dollars. Worse than a goddamned woman. Motherfuck this dog.* He put on his hat, found a piece of newsprint blown against the chainlink fence around the car lot, and used it to wipe the blood off his hands, then reeled off into the darkness.

The light inside the bar was faint and gray and left the vague shadow of the door edge on the crumbled stoop. Flies descended upon the dumpster to snarl and buzz about the dog carcass. Morrison took the .38 from his belt where his shirt hung untucked, then imagined the dog dying in the dirt pit, surrounded by the horrible laughter of drunk men, its throat ripped open and an eye lying sightless in the paw-printed dirt before the four legs suddenly caved. He looked over at the car lot. His last sight was a Pinto for five hundred dollars and marked sold, maybe bought by a Mexican who thought he could fix the car when it broke down. He thumbed back the hammer and took a deep breath before he walked through the doorway. This was the end.

Jesus Pagan was obese and alone behind the horseshoe bar straightening and counting the sweaty bills that he made into three piles as if he were a blackjack dealer. The two pool tables against the wall were made level by pieces of cinder block. He wore no shirt and his hairy stomach kept him inches from the bar ledge. An electric fan next to him turned and sluiced through the air that had been breathed many times and blew against his unshaven face. Hair sprouted from his nose. Jesus did not look up from his counting. There was the tattoo of a lion under a thicket of arm hair.

I told you niggers no more dogs tonight, he said.

Morrison stood in the dark bar with the pistol drawn. There was nobody coming. It was only the fat man with wet chest hair stuck together in small twists. He was counting to himself and moving his lips without words. A half-eaten hamburger lay on the wrapper, the fries doused in catsup.

Your dog dies, your dog motherfucking dies. One dog always does. Now fuck off and get out.

Jesus still had not looked up from the neat piles of bills.

Morrison's reflection was distorted in the cracked barback mirror. He leveled the .38 at himself and fired three rounds. Jesus dropped behind the bar. Morrison waited for him to rise up firing, but nothing moved except the electric fan blowing the bills all over the filthy tile floor. He heard Jesus panting drool with deep, asthmatic heaves, then put the pistol back in his pants and walked out the door down the alley.

*The pigeons flew crazily between the streetlamp posts while the scrawny whore gave Mateo a hand-job in the warehouse doorway. Morrison watched from the squad parked in the alley mouth off Lake and Damen. The whore was wide-eyed from dope, her arms thin, bulged with veins. Mateo leaned back against the brick wall with his uniform pants down to his knees.*

*Oh bitch, he said. You sure know how to hold a cock. Now show me your titties, dirty girl. Show me how you'd like to suck up my cock.*

*The whore lifted up her shirt and put Mateo's finger into her mouth while he masturbated. The morning was still dark. Morrison smoked a cigarette, the sallow sky congealing between the housing projects, when the dispatcher put on Sergeant Jimmy Wills to read the news that Saigon had fallen: To all former jarheads and doggie pricks on the Chicago PD–let me say my brothers that the Nam was a bust, one big shit in the shorts. A motherfucking waste worse than leaving prime poon-tang out in the rain. Do you read me? The gooks got Saigon and we got the big, green weenie right up our assholes. Thanks for the memories, Victor Charles, you rat-eating cocksucker.*

*Morrison snuffed the cigarette on the dash. He felt sick to his stomach because there was nothing else to feel. He tried giving a shit, but all that came were the wet, peaceful faces of the marines he shot and his resentment that they were out of it forever. None of them would have to forget a thing, or try not remembering what they saw with their eyes.*

*The small rain misted the windshield and smeared the streetlights. Morrison watched the whore stumble away down the alley. The pigeons whirred their vernacular and fluttered away from her staggering. Mateo grinned when he got inside the squad, then drank back a cold cup of thermos coffee.*

*Wills just called that Saigon fell, Morrison said. The NVA got the whole thing now.*

*I was drafted, Mateo said. I could give two shits about what happens to those gook motherfuckers. I was there in 1971. Nobody gave a shit then.*

Morrison drove up the alley and the tires popped the bottle glass. He passed the whore, sunk to her ankles in a puddle boiled by the rain. Her face was wasted and soaked. Mateo tapped his fingers on the dash to some salsa rhythm.

*I could never get into fucking a gook, Mateo said. Small tits. Little pussy. There was nothing to them.*

The raindrops peened off the squad's hood. The whore was still in the puddle, hazed by the rain. She walked in circles and looked skyward. Morrison hit the accelerator and the squad went bouncing over the potholes.

*I always felt like a child molester with them gooks, Mateo said. You know how they all looked twelve fucking years old. Their mouths were never big enough to suck good cock. Some guys got into that shit, but not me. But you know who liked it? The white officers. The college pricks running the show. Them guys thought banging a gook was the best fucking there was. Says something about white broads, doesn't it?*

Morrison drove the alley behind some vacant storefronts with one-room flats on the second floor. Squalls of rain went driving into three dumpsters chained together at the wheels and overflowing with garbage. The plastic bags had been gored by pigeon's beaks. Mateo was singing Spanish along with his tapping when his eyes darted toward the dumpsters. He went silent and sucked air so that teeth sounded in his breath. Morrison stopped the squad.

*Keep on going, Mateo said.*

*What did you see?*

*Just drive.*

Morrison reversed and then opened the window and stuck his head out into the rain to see. The alley gave way to an empty lot. There was nothing in front of the dumpster but a slashed mattress and a vinyl chair. He worked the spotlight against the wet buildings while Mateo breathed in cadence with the swinging wiper blades. Then Morrison saw a wet foot with painted nails, lightly mud-stained, sticking out from behind the dumpster.

Just because you see it, Mateo said, don't mean you got to see it. Let's keep on going. It don't mean nothing.

Morrison left the foot in the spotlight beam and radioed for an ambulance, almost forgetting the call number for this scene. Mateo stared away at the foul dawn coming over the power lines and rooftops of the West Side.

I ain't looking at that shit, he said. And I ain't touching nothing.

Morrison got out of the squad like he hadn't heard him. Inside, Mateo was shaking, even sweating cold; for him, being a cop was only an opportunity to steal. Morrison walked around the hood with his drawn service revolver, his legs briefly awash in the headlights. He kicked away the tattered mattress as two rats went running off along the building's wall. The springs stuck through the fabric and bloodstains smeared the exposed stuffing. He smelled maggots and rotting chicken bones and the shit from diapers.

The pale woman lay behind the dumpster on the gravel and broken glass. Her eyes were swollen from punches. The rain straightened her pubic hair, as if cleansing the mottle of semen and dirt. She hummed a song that Morrison recognized but could not name.

Tears warped his sight when he bent down to touch her throat. He felt a weak pulse that sent waves back through his body. The woman was looking at him, unblinking. She was naked and shivering, cut about her breasts and stomach. They'd slit her wrists, though not deep enough to kill her. He holstered his service revolver, took off his leather jacket, and covered her with it. Then he lay down beside the woman as if her lover while the sirens from the ambulance drew closer. Her breath was vague. She trembled. He hummed the unknown song with her and in a deep place felt very much in love, perhaps more in love than he had ever been.

**T**he two blacks on the stoop stopped drinking malt liquor when Jack Tyne climbed the steps of the Viceroy Hotel. They shared a forty-ounce bottle wrapped in a brown paper bag and were too drunk to hold up their heads. The Chicago air was a hot collage of gunned engines and radio music and an invisible grime that Jack felt in his pores like glue. He was neither home nor in the army. Nothing else mattered.

One black wore a baseball cap decorated with sequins and plastic jewels. He pitched the empty bottle so that it burst on the sidewalk. Jack breathed slow and pressed the buzzer when he found it; the sound came after a short delay. The men started another bottle and drank without words. There was no sound except for their swallowing.

When he looked through the glass doors, a man rose
from a green couch and hobbled across the lobby tiles on
twisted legs. He opened the door and stood looking out, a
milky crust about his lips. The blacks drank in long swigs
and green flies took turns landing on their eyelids. The
two were half-gone, reeling where they sat as if driftwood
on the banks of a summer river, gnatty, rife with rot. The
man looked at Jack with drink-galled eyes and scratched
his coarse chest hair through a worn T-shirt.

Any rooms? Jack said.

The man bore his long fingernails hard into his chest.
His fly was undone.

Day, week, what? he said.

A week to start, Jack said.

It's forty now and twenty for the sheets, he said. You
get it back if you don't fuck them up. There ain't no cur-
few but sometimes I sleep through the bell. If I do, you're
just plain-ass fucked.

The man opened the door further and sized Jack up
with his colorless eyes. The blacks were gape-mouthed,
staring up at him like baby birds waiting for a worm.

I told you niggers to fuck off, he said.

They did not move.

Dumb sons of bitches, he said. Stupid niggers can't
even fuck off. Come on inside, kid.

The lobby smelled like hot garbage and ran up to a
metal staircase at the back of the room. There were folding chairs, a green vinyl sofa, smoke rising from a stand-
up ashtray. The coffee table was stacked high with newspapers and Coke cans from the pop machine in the corner
that boasted *tough shit on refunds*. One chair was heaped
with folded linen and the other held a small TV with a
bent coat hanger for an antenna. The ten o'clock news had
just started with a story about a big house fire in progress;
the black children hammed in the camera shot and danced
while the reporter tried to read the facts.

The man sat heavily on the couch. His shaved head

was flecked with tiny scars. He seemed happy that Jack was a white man.

All these niggers got to do is get smart and they'd take the whole fucking works, he said.

There's a lot of them around, Jack said.

Assloads. There's more fucking niggers than pigeons. But the thing you got to do is figure out how to make money off them. A young guy like you should think about that.

Jack looked up from the floor. A clear ooze had hardened on the tiles.

But it ain't easy making money off a nigger, the man said. You got to be around them all day and they always want to see the manager about something. But shit, they'll buy about anything you tell them they need. It don't matter. They'll spend their last ten bucks on the most useless bullshit and seem happy as hell. Niggers are like that. If you could get a couple good ones working for you, you'd really have something. That's the trick.

What's the trick?

Finding a couple good ones. The women are the best but they'll spread their legs for a hamburger and are always getting knocked up.

Jack traded the man three twenty-dollar bills for the linen. It was yellowed and smelled of old ashtrays. The man gave him the room key from a strong box sitting next to him on the couch. Liver spots and wonky moles dotted the crown of his head. He started coughing like a dog trying to vomit. Jack wanted to ask where the room was, but tears flung from the man's eyes as he swallowed and hacked harder. The man pointed with his thumb behind himself, up the stairs, vaguely saying IE as if his mouth were full of gravel. He did not stop coughing.

The room was no more than a big closet with a cot and a sink that had been painted white. The thin mattress where Jack set down his bag from the army was full of cigarette burns. The neon sign blinked red through the closed blinds, then hard into his eyes when he opened them. For the first time in his life, he could not see the stars and the moon because of the city lights reflecting in the pollution haze. There were only the drunks out with their bottles, dirty-lipped, red-eyed, haggard men like the cast-off mannequins in department store dumpsters. They drank openly from bottles of cold wine as if the city itself were an endless tavern. Drunks were everywhere, seated on bus stop benches, the steps of storefront churches, car hoods that were not their own. Jack tried looking above these reeling winos off to poke in the alley trash but could not see beyond the rooftops. The city was stranger than all of his dreams, and within its constant drone he hoped to escape not only the wasted corn, but himself and his memories.

Jack walked over to the little cot, tore off his T-shirt, and sat on the thin mattress, then lay back and propped his feet up on the iron rail. The sky had darkened with rainless clouds. He kicked off his boots. He covered his eyes with the folded linen. *Without his love, Gina? What love have you ever seen enough to know?* That night he dreamed of thin lightning wires flashing without sound above the wrecked cornfields until the rain came and flooded the stalks up to their tassels. He sweated and turned many times in his sleep, but never once did he wake and look about the room, wondering where he was.

He slept through the next morning and it was already near dusk when he rose from the small cot and found the communal shower down the hallway. Three shower heads stuck out of the wall and there was a backed-up stool behind a metal divider. Wet toilet paper was stuck to the ceiling. He left his tennis shoes on against the filth. He washed alone with his back against the wall and did not take long.

That night he sat on the stoop drinking a Coke and smoking a cigarette from the last pack he'd bought at Fort Bragg. *Fuck the army.* When he snuffed the butt on the step, a fight spilled out of the hotel doors and two men

with eyes bulged from drunken meanness went rolling
down the stoop. Their faces jerked from the clumsy jabs,
and shiny gouts of blood fell from their mouths. Jack rose
to his feet and made way while a nip-faced man seized up
the face of a guy with squirrel teeth and bit it. He kicked
and tossed. Nipface then gave a hard pull as if to tear off
the most cheek he could before turning him loose and
running crazily down the sidewalk. The wounded man
held his cheek with a hand and gave chase, the blood
spewing from between his fingers.

A young black followed the fighters out on the stoop
and stood looking after them with Jack. He was tall and
thick-necked, his T-shirt pulled tight over finely chiseled
chest muscles and biceps. His eyes were kind and large
when he looked at Jack and he smiled so wide that they
almost closed. They laughed together when a nappy-
headed drunk poked along the sidewalk with the gait of a
dog with three paws, perhaps looking for cigarette butts
in the gutter long enough to straighten and relight. The
black offered him a Kool when the drunk staggered off
and Jack took it.

Thanks, he said.

Ain't nothing.

They lit the cigarettes and sat down. Jack didn't know if
the black was looking at him, or just plain looking.

Crazy sons of bitches, the black said of the fighters.

Last night I saw them drinking together, Jack said.
They were arm in arm right there in the curb.

It sometimes starts that way. It sometimes ends like
that too.

They smoked the menthol cigarettes and blew the
smoke out into the last of the daylight, leaning back on one
hand.

Herman says you're looking for work, the black said.

Who's Herman?

The goofy motherfucker who runs the hotel. That
horny bastard has every dirty book there is. He's always

Washington Free Public Library
120 East Main St.
Washington, IA 52353

back there beating his shit off. I bet he ain't on the couch watching his game shows.

The black exaggerated his nodding. Jack looked at him.

Go on, he said. I bet if you went to the bathroom, that shit would be locked tight.

I'll take your word on that one, Jack said.

The black shook his head in laughter. He held his cigarette more than he smoked it.

So you need a job? he said.

Nothing in a kitchen, Jack said. I'm not that broke.

I'm with you there. Kitchen work is worse than motherfucking jail. You got all these spics running around talking you down in Mexican because a nigger like me don't know what they're saying. There really ain't no white man who hates a nigger more than a Mexican does. But when Hector and Juan get to drinking, they almost worse than a church bus full of black people who got the holy ghost. You ever see a bunch of niggers singing about Jesus?

No, Jack said.

There ain't no future in it. Any goddamned way, my name's Blake. My momma named me after some white man on a soap opera.

My name's Jack. My ma named me after my father.

Your last name ain't Meoff, is it? Blake said. I saw this movie once where these silly white boys call this bowling alley and have Jack Meoff paged.

No, Jack said. But you aren't the first to ask.

Where you from in the world?

Watega County. Downstate. I just got out of the army.

A country motherfucker turned GI Joe. What you turning into next?

Anything but what I was.

I'm just trying to stay away from the crazy niggers I come up with, Blake said. But you like moving?

Jack looked at him, then flung his butt in the street.

You know, Blake said. Moving white people from the city all the way up to the North Shore.

They need guys?

They always need guys. It's like the army that way. The work gets so hot that niggers even faint.

Shit.

Ain't no time to shit, white man. We got to get the blond womens moved.

Does it pay?

Nothing like this pays. You just can't be a drunk like most of the white men who wash up here.

I've noticed that, Jack said.

They are the kind who hate a nigger the most. The rich man doesn't even have to know we live. But being white is all those poor motherfuckers got.

I was in the army with a few like that.

I bet you were, Blake said. I was in the marines with all of their cousins.

The next morning they came up Grand Avenue from the east in the dark before the dawn, past the barred dollar stores and the hot dog stands where come daylight the poor would whir like flies. Jack and Blake walked abreast on the sidewalk.

What did you do in the marines? Jack said.

I drove a truck and fought crackers and counted the motherfucking days.

Shit.

What did you do? Blake said.

I was a paratrooper.

There ain't but two things that fall from the sky—birdshit and fools. I never took you for either one.

Jack grinned.

In four years, he said, I never saw falling birdshit, but I saw a lot of fools. You ever miss the marines?

Blake's soft, ebony face already glowed with sweat.

You ever miss having the shits?

They went laughing up the street to the truck lot of the moving company where windswept garbage clung against the slanted barbed wire atop the chainlink fence. The trucks sat in their shadows cast by streetlight pale as milk, the gate locked with a heavy chain roped between the poles. Blacks milled by the gate or sat in the curb already eating the sandwiches from their sack lunches. The men wore sweatpants and T-shirts with cut-off sleeves and many had leather weightlifting belts around their waists. The gelled hair of the young men shone in the morning dark. Jack and Blake came to stand among this group and Jack looked for another white face. He found none and was eyed with a rage and anger he'd never quite known. He felt like lunch on a plate. The smell of reefer and sweet wine was general and the men smoking joints made no effort to hide them.

Blake spat and wiped his lips with his arm, then regarded his fellows. He drew his eyes. His thick frame assumed the pose of a boxer being read the rules. He eyed them all as if his stare could impale.

This man's with me, Blake said.

Brotherhood run deep, a coal-faced black said.

Look at the gray motherfucker, said a skinny kid with wild hair. Maybe he's just a nigger fell in bleach.

Jack's bowels twitched as he stepped closer to Blake.

This man is with me, Blake said. I ain't telling you again.

There was a trailer in the back of the truck lot and the shadows of the paper bags blown against the fence were cast by the streetlight against its corrugated wall. The door opened and a man came outside speaking Polish with someone still inside the trailer. The blacks crowded the gate and waited, eyeing Blake and Jack as if they'd carve off their noses with broken bottles. Across the street men were arriving late in long cars with rusted fenders, visquine for windows, even red crepe paper standing in for brake lights. The Pole moved among his trucks with the slowness of summer dusk, then unlocked the swing gate with a key tied to his belt. He was a short man dressed in second-hand clothes. Under his armpit was a .45 auto-matic in a shoulder holster. He unwound the shiny chain with a cigarette dangling from the corner of his mouth, standing in a way so that all the men could see the pistol. His thin lips were as unsmiling as a dog's. He looked out at the black faces with disgust.

Blake and Jack were the last to file inside the lot where the battered Ford 1000 trucks were parked with bug guts splattered on the windshields. A jerri-curled black with marijuana breath walked beside Jack, scoping him with bug eyes before taking things from his pocket: a Zippo lighter, a gold chain, a fake Rolex with rhinestone inlay, two chocolate bars in various stages of melt. He made his white palms into a kind of table and held out his wares for Jack to see.

What's up, the black said.

Nothing, said Jack. He saw Blake shaking his head.

You don't see nothing here you want? the black said.

No.

You don't see nothing here you want to buy?

Not a thing.

You smoke blunts? the black said.

I don't know what the hell that is, Jack said.

Here, the black said.

He put everything back into his pockets and took out a bag of small cigars hollowed out and filled with pot.

Now these here are some blunts, he said.

Blake put an unlit cigarette in his mouth and stepped between them.

Leave this man to his business, he said.

I'm just making my services available, the black said.

Nigger get a clue, Blake said.

The men lolled by their trucks and ate Twinkies and pork rinds from plastic bags. They were already broken down into crews of three and awaited work assignments. Some folded furniture blankets and coiled ropes in a slop-py way and laughed loudly about the shine from Jack's white face. An old black with a white beard hobbled about the trucks testing the air pressure of the tires by swinging a club against their worn treads. The younger men called him Uncle Billy, Uncle Tom, or just old goat-looking motherfucker.

The Pole grabbed Jack by the arm and snorted a laugh so that his nostril hairs fell from his nose. He eyed Jack for a long second, then wiped his nose with the back of his hand. The .45 automatic was loud beneath his sweaty armpit. Blake had gone off by his truck to smoke alone away from the younger men who played grab-ass all over the truck lot. There was a bit of Wilder about him, Jack thought, the man who just wanted to do his job and be left alone. The Pole smiled and nodded his fat head.

You are a hard-luck boy, he said to Jack.

Jack said nothing.

All alone with blackie, he said. You have real hard luck.

I was just hoping to work, Jack said.

We try you, but you won't last. You won't come back after today. You'll go crazy working with blackie. He fucks around like a little boy and only works for wine and dope.

The Pole cocked an eye at Jack, as if surprised that he was still standing there. He smelled like a wet dog.

All the white boys that come here are drunks and fuckups, he said. They never come back the second day. This work is for blackie, and it's blackie who knows how to do it. No white boy has made it yet.

I'll work with Blake, Jack said. Everything will be all right.

Then go over there and pray for your luck, the Pole said. But I don't see you tomorrow. I know this.

Blake was sitting on the truck's running board with a black named Arthur who emptied a bag of hotskins into his mouth when Jack walked up. Blake smiled and patted his shoulder. Arthur was very quiet, as if wrapped in his own atmosphere. He wore sunglasses in the dark and had a jailhouse tough way about crunching the hotskins.

Niggers are like this, Blake said. It'll be cool by the afternoon. They're just pissed off because you ain't been doing this shit as long as they have.

Jack looked at his boot toes while Arthur let the bag fall from his hands.

We're all scratching here, Blake said. There ain't no man among us who ain't.

I know it.

Then let it all go.

Why are you different? Jack said.

With me, it's just people. A black man will go crazy in his head thinking any other way because he'll keep coming back to himself as being a nigger. It ain't no way to live. Right, Arthur?

Arthur stared up at the dark skies from behind his sunglasses.

I don't care about nothing, he said, but fucking some bitches. You know, really knocking the lining out of them. That's all that counts.

From the east the sallow light leaked over the city when they pulled out of the truck lot. The truck Blake drove slipped gears and took the potholes so hard that the sideview mirrors fell down away from sight. Arthur sat low beside the window and beat raps with his fist against the outside of the truck door. *Your woman playing you like a wild jack.* He sneered at his own reflection in the windshield glass while the daylight broke the hot darkness over the rooftops of West Side three-flats, as if his pose boasted his early release from Joliet after serving just two of his four years for armed robbery. He was short but lethal. Jack rode in the middle, through these wrecked neighborhoods washed with pigeon shit and the dust scum from so many rainless days.

Shut your mouth, Arthur, Blake said. I don't want to hear that shit.

Arthur stopped singing but continued banging on the outside of the truck door. He tilted his head back and feigned sleep.

All those songs do is make niggers act like a bunch of fools, Blake said. I bet it was some rap that made you wave that zip gun in the Arab's face and make off with 134 bucks. The Man had incarceration waiting for your ass and the silly nigger singing them songs just got paid. Whatever happened to Marvin Gaye? No motherfucker ever did anything but get busy after hearing him sing.

That nigger's old man wasted him, Arthur said. Popped him with a Dirty Harry gun. That's what the fuck happened to Marvin Gaye.

I'm just saying that you must miss the jailhouse. With your attitude, that Mexican parole officer will have you back in Stateville denims with a drop seat.

Hell no, Arthur said. I give the black snake. I don't take it. I give it to some fat polack.

Who talks his English worse than twenty country niggers, Blake said.

No, Arthur said. A hundred drunk Chinamen.

Blake stopped at a red light and howled with laughter. Arthur eyed a young black girl waiting for a bus on a bench. She wore white plastic beads in her long braids. The bus jarred along the curb through the exhaust fume, its air brakes farting loudly. The girl stared past Arthur, down the busy street, popping her bubble gum. He looked at her sideways through his dark glasses, working his tongue against his lips as if to let her see that he could already taste her.

Hey girl, Arthur said.

The girl turned and gave him a mean face. Her eyes hard as marble, her skin light chocolate.

Look at this bitch, Arthur said.

She's smart enough to look through your ass, Blake said.

Shit, Arthur said. He smelled of marijuana and coconut oil.

Blake smiled at Jack who was also watching the girl even though he was not part of it. He thought she might be pregnant the way she covered her stomach with a shopping bag.

Where we going on Fullerton? Blake said to Jack.

He drove and pointed to the work order on the clipboard without watching himself.

Right there, he said.

625 West, Jack said. Third floor.

Where to?

To meet the motherfucking Man, Arthur said. That's all who's there.

Nigger, Blake said, you must be missing your incarceration real bad today.

Time ain't shit, Arthur said. Niggers run the show inside.

That's something to cry about, Blake said.

If you're locked-up and white, Arthur said.

I think we are going to Winnetka, Jack said.

Motherfuck, Jacky, Blake said. Two niggers and a corn-fed white boy are delivering the American Dream today for eight dollars an hour plus a motherfucking nontaxable tip.

Jack smiled.

Yessir, Blake said. Being a nigger is an interesting life.

Then there was the clean air. It came within ten blocks. Where the sunlight had glared white in the pollution haze above the fenced used car lots and bulletproof currency exchanges, there was now clean, blue sky and cafés and bookshops and statues of great men in parks beside flower beds with pumping sprinklers and the azure water of Lake Michigan that rose at the horizon so that Jack did not know where the lake stopped and the sky began. It was wonderful summer all through the streets lined with oaks and maples and ivy-covered graystones where beautiful white women walked the sidewalks with the aloof pose of runway models in blouses sheer enough to show the lace of their bras.

Blake turned the truck down side streets where German cars with square grills were parked tightly along the curbs. The bay windows of townhouses were lined with stained glass that caught the sunlight like the insides of a kaleidoscope. Arthur stared down joggers and dog walkers and men in suits with newspapers folded neatly under their arms, even the young women who lilted and floated like Jack's fantasies about them. His stare was meant to terrify this world with the brutal sadness of another one only ten blocks away, but it was missed by these people of the cool lake wind because they would never have to know they should be frightened by it.

The blond couple came down the front stairs of a three-flat graystone with their coffee while Blake was double-parking the truck. The man was thin and soft-looking and the woman was quiet in the way of a big mother cat. They wore oversized Northwestern University T-shirts and khaki shorts. There was a cleanliness to them that Jack hated. He just wanted to see the guy bloodied a little bit, the kind look knocked off his face with a hard left hook. He kept looking at his wife through his glasses and she was all business, no joke to her face.

Yessir, Blake said. This is Mike and Megan, or Jim and Anne, or Brian and Jennifer, or some damned shit like that. Maybe even Elliot and Rachel. She'd cut your nuts off. He'd just look at you and tell you how cool everything is. He'll try helping us a little bit. Maybe get us a fucking hamburger from McDonalds.

Blake sighed while Jack laughed.

We ain't nothing but niggers and white trash to them, Blake said. Big pieces of shit. I bet he ain't never been in a fight and she ain't never cum once in her life. She hates him for it, too.

I'd grab that bitch's ears and fuck her in the ass, Arthur said.

You just keep your thug ass right there until we get going, Blake said to Arthur. I don't want you mind-fucking that woman all day and ruining the tip.

Arthur nodded and drowsed off with the peace of a man who can lie down anywhere and fall asleep. Blake smiled at Jack while he put a tin of brown shoe polish in his pocket, then wiped the sweat off his face with his hand.

What's the shoe polish for? Jack said.

To cover up all the places where we gouge their furniture.

Son of a bitch, Jack said.

There's lots of tricks a nigger learns to get a tip out of a white man. Shit, Jacky. Arthur will be in the truck getting anything I miss. But there's one thing I don't understand about these kind of white men.

What's that?

How rich they are, but how stupid they look.

In the truck lot the pay line was formed in the dark and the blacks smoked menthol cigarettes down to their filters. They were a raw lot, dressed in loose jeans, their faces and T-shirts marbled with sweat and dirt. The oldest men among them stood as if they were leaned against a lightpost and looked nowhere with sunken eyes, perhaps dreaming of a life beyond day labor or already adding the wages from the long hours to spend on big-legged women in the lounges of the West Side. The young men were lithe like great cats, long and sinewy, with veins bulging from their arms, and eyes that sought weakness as the only opportunity they would ever have.

Jack and Blake got out of the truck through the driver's door. A white-bearded black set a step stool on the gravel, climbed up the front bumper, and opened the hood. He checked the oil dipstick with a flashlight and wiped it clean with an old T-shirt. His knees were crooked in his pants and a truss was wrapped around his waist. Arthur was slumped against the window with half-closed eyes, lost in the profane rap, *I want to fuck you in the ass.*

We got to get our place, Blake said. We're on the last truck as it is.

How long do we have to wait? Jack said.

Until this polack motherfucker has a buzz enough to forget he spends his days with niggers.

Where is he?

In the trailer drinking beer with four polacks fatter than he is.

They walked to the line and Jack ignored the hard stares by watching the sky for rain and hoping that when it came, it would fall cold for days. The young men rapped and clapped and passed around forty-ounce malt liquor bottles as if they were joints. Arthur danced his dance among them, having come awake at quitting time to fall easily into the way of things. Jack and Blake took their place at the end behind a fat black not much older than them with sweaty jowls and the darkest skin of any man in the line. His gold front teeth caught the light of the truck lot pole lamps. He looked at Jack, blew two thin streams of smoke from his nose, and nodded, dropping an empty Coke can. On the outside of his wrist was the tattoo of a top hat and a cane inside of a star.

Born and bred West Side, my brother, he said to Blake.

Blake laughed in his face. He mocked the hard eyes of a drill sergeant.

Charles, he said. You are an offense to the sunshine.

You an offense to the race. You tom motherfucker.

I ain't running, fat man.

They teach you to kill in the marines? Charles said. Because you going to have to kill me.

Nigger, quit making promises.

Charles clenched his fists and let his bloated arms dangle. He had breasts like a woman. Limp nipples the size of silver dollars showed through his sweaty T-shirt.

I got all my damned life if you want some of this, he said.

With titties like you got, Blake said, I don't know if I should fight you or fuck you.

Arthur passed off the malt liquor, moved behind

Charles, and smiled bone white teeth while he mimed sodomy, humping the air like a dumb dog. The men went dipshit with laughter. A black with his head in a shower cap fell down from laughing so hard and broke the malt liquor bottle against a truck fender. Some yellow-skinned kid spread out his hands and feigned a grope of Charles' D-cup breasts as the fat man took off after him through the hoops of light. His cushy ass bounced. His hard breath sounded in the darkness. He wore down very quickly and stood panting by the gate with his hands on his sloppy hips. Long drops of snot and drool fell from his mouth and nose.

The Pole came from the trailer, dropped his cigarette into an empty beer can, and set the can on the ground, then crushed it end to end. He bent a smile and stared balefully at the pay line before spitting on the gravel. His countrymen followed him outside and opened fresh beers. They spoke in Polish between bursts of drunken laughter, the three of them, their red Slavic faces pointed as icicles. Their faded work clothes were stained with axle grease and house paint. The Pole took the roll of cash from his pocket and undid the rubberband holding it together. The blacks assumed the urgent pose of dogs at the promise of meat scraps.

You, the Pole said, pointing to Jack.

Jack looked at him from the back of the line. His heart was pounding and his mouth turned dry.

Yes, you, said the Pole. I look your way. Come get your money, hard-luck boy.

Somewhere in the street beyond the truck lot fence, the bell from an ice cream vendor's pushcart rang along the sidewalk. A dog barked. Jack Tyne understood that he could not have heard these things unless every voice in the line had quieted. The men eyed him cruelly. He looked at Blake, who was looking at his ripped basketball shoes.

The Pole smiled like a jerk cop.

You don't want your money? he said.

Jack stepped forward and his shadow came with him out of the larger shadow of the truck. The men put cigarettes in their mouths, lit them, and smoked in the dusk. One black with an open shirt and a gang brand on his chest spat a mouthful of malt liquor at Jack. The Pole stood in the hooped light like a perverse vaudevillian and held out the bills for Jack.

How many hours you work? he said.

Ten.

You're not bullshitting me.

No, Jack said. I worked ten hours.

Because the blackies are full of bullshit. They always have shit in their mouths. They always have shit to talk. I think that maybe you ate some of their shit with a spoon.

He glared at Jack. His face was wet and his eyes were almost all red from drinking beer in the heat.

What's wrong, hard-luck boy? he said.

Jack said nothing.

Even with the hard luck, you are still a white man, the Pole said. That is still better than being blackie with a thousand dollars.

Jack took the folded bills as if being handed cat shit. It came to eighty dollars.

There's something extra, the Pole said. I make you a lucky boy. The map of Poland is on your face.

They all broke into throaty laughter.

You come back tomorrow, lucky boy. I need you to keep the rest in line. I will make you a big boss.

He slapped Jack on the shoulder, hard with an open hand, then waved for the blacks to receive their pay. They lined up with downturned eyes and took their money and shoved the bills into their pockets without counting them. Jack walked off and waited for Blake by the fence, leaning on his heels against the chainlink and watching the blacks pass out of the gate dripping sweat from their eyelids. Some walked off with half limps to a liquor store beyond Chicago Avenue where Mexican kids sat drinking pop on parked cars, souped-up Vegas and Pintos with tinted windows and tire rims and slimeburst paint jobs worth more than the cars themselves. The old men took off baseball hats for the wind to cool their foreheads, gashed from wrinkles, before disappearing into tap rooms or idling buses or the great sallow darkness beyond. None of them paid this lone white boy any mind now. Their thoughts were set on the binges or fuck-fests to come, the day to forget.

Jack and Blake walked silently down alleys back to the Viceroy Hotel. The darkness was white where the street appeared between the tumbledown three-flats. Jack watched while Blake made animals with the shadow of his hand against a garage wall. Then he raised his arms to stretch them and worked his neck around with wide circles.

Being a nigger is sure some weird shit, he said.

I wouldn't know, Jack said.

Ain't nothing to know. It just is.

Jack offered Blake half a candy bar but he waved it away with his hand.

You can't trust blacks no more than you trust whites, Blake said. Most niggers want to prove that they are the blackest motherfucker in the world. Whites either look right through your ass or tell you how sorry they are for everything.

Sorry for what? Jack said.

You know, how fucked up it is being a nigger.

This black guy in the army named Felder told me that much, Jack said. He seemed alone even when he was with other black people.

I know that feeling. Also, it ain't often that a nigger gets to hate a white boy right out in the open.

Jack was silent.

Some of them have been waiting all their lives for you to come around today. It ain't no good. You just have to look at people and guess if they're okay or not. That's all you can really do.

I'm not very good at that.

Ain't nobody good at guessing, Blake said. You just got to pick a number.

Jack looked down the alley that ran without end and offered Blake a cigarette and they lit them off the same match in his cupped hand.

he doors of the Primitive Baptist Church were propped open to the hot night by old tire rims, and a west wind blew in the reek from the burst garbage bags scattered in the vacant lot across the street. Morrison sat on the curb, looking straight inside the storefront church whenever the red light turned green that held still the cars with thumping music and tinted windows. His eyes were inflamed with wind-borne grit. The congregation was decorated for Sunday on Friday night in white dresses and purple zoot suits and they took turns at the pulpit holding the microphone to sing. *What? What would I do? What would I do without Jesus?* Their words were garbled by the fan blades that spun in the windows over the alley.

The whole congregation was dancing with wide eyes and wet faces. The fat matrons gyrated faster than the rate of the music coming from a band of teenage boys behind the pulpit, then collapsed in fits, fainting backward into the ramshackle pews to pant like paranoids the vernacular of God. The band played on: a bass, keyboards, a four-piece drum set, the players stiff as ice. The women's floral dresses were wrung wet and clung to tired wombs. Adolescent boys in cheap suits fanned them back into consciousness with shy and scared looks, nappy heads, one or two eyeing the alley dark beyond the church doors, perhaps dreaming of escape into its shadows as if they understood that Cain was not Abel nor would he ever be. The coal-faced elders in white robes swayed and clapped with restraint under the houselights fiercer than the noonday sun, giving each and every supplicant their two minutes to sing variations on a single line. *You can't look back once Jesus turns you around.*

Morrison watched the faithful and sipped the Scotch in slow mouthfuls. The main aisle of the church was soon clogged with dancers, sweaty female necks with strings of fake pearls, young girls with plastic beads braided into their hair, young boys moving their legs and arms, so mannered and intricate.

He took a breath and looked at his large hands as if their lines and callouses marked the way back home. *Don't let nobody turn you off Jesus.* His chest ached. He knew the sickness would come bad if he did not find the man with the Delta 88 and the bum leg, so he stood and walked with his bottle past a little black girl on a three-flat stoop. She wore pigtails and danced the teasing dance of a belly dancer, then jumped and crossed and recrossed her legs before her bare feet touched the cement. He wiped his eyes and set off down the street bouncing off parked cars and trying to keep fixed on some orange glow many blocks away. It moved when he moved.

On Ashland Avenue, Morrison braced himself against a parking meter and retched into the sewer grate in the lights of the few passing cars . Morrison cursed or spat or even ran after them, the teenagers tightly packed into customized Caprices with joints and forty-ounce bottles. One car slowed and reversed and pelted him with bottles and rocks while tears warped his sight. The flying debris scared pigeons off the dumpster lids. The birds dissolved into the darkness like the car. Morrison's face was wet from vomit and cold sweat.

He wandered a web of alleys and walked as if his knees did not bend. In a dirty wind near the Lake Street El, Morrison found a young black man lying belly down on the alley rocks beneath a warehouse truck dock. The back pockets were ripped from his jeans. Morrison watched him for a minute to see if he was dead. He kicked gravel at him, then a beer can, a piece of broken cinder block. The black reached for a handhold in the night air, his hair all caught with grit. Morrison staggered closer. He could see where his eyes had been stove shut with a board, and he could see the blood coming from them in thin streams. The black's slack mouth twisted. His head moved as if he were trying to look over his shoulder. Morrison took the .38 from his belt and backed off around a telephone pole, seeing three bodies where he knew there was one, when he tripped backward and squeezed off a round from pure fear. The sound of the report was soon lost to the dark blocks.

His eyes twitched when he sat up and found his legs over a lanky white boy. He rolled off of him. The boy stirred heavily, his cheeks all pocked with gravel. Morrison knelt, then vomited sour bile on the boy's soldier haircut. He could see the lean muscles of his back beneath his thin T-shirt and his ribs heaving from breath. Morrison touched him. The boy rolled to his side. Drool fell from his mouth. His eyes seemed to open from the sides like a cat's inner lids and his eye whites were choked with red. He moaned suddenly, the reek of Morrison's vomit coming off him. His lips drew back over bloody teeth. He swallowed, perhaps thinking he spoke.

Morrison rose up and stumbled backward and sat down heavily on a stack of cardboard boxes. Then he got up again. He stood reeling and staring at the boy through his cloudy eyes. *Son of a bitch.* His eyes were casting about. Seeing the pistol still in his hand, he shoved it inside his belt. There was a swath in the loose gravel where they had drug this boy by the ankles. The black lay motionless on his stomach, his butt cheeks poking through the ripped-out pockets of his blue jeans. Morrison turned away, then took a step forward, his eyes fixed on this white boy's face all wet and gray-looking from the night, the memories coming like gut shots.

*The wounded marines lay with their intestines roped around the rubble after Morrison shot them. None of them were moaning. There were no cries to be thin and lost in the wind. He blinked his eyes three times as if that would clear this sight from his head. They all lay with big smiles in the rain like ocean waves or the wide peaks of mountains. The platoon stood and filed off in two columns behind the tanks while the rain hissed and steamed off the hot gun barrels. Morrison fell into the rear of the soaked formation and readied his rifle to continue forever this march through cities and over landscapes not yet dreamed. But he swore he remained with the men he had shot, enough so that he even watched himself walk off.*

Morrison had run off about a block from the white boy and the black before he stopped again. He stood there in the alley staring back at the boy, his face buried in the dust and city bracken, dry-heaving. Morrison took his own face in his hands and pinched as if squeezing all the water out of a sponge. *Son of a bitch. Nothing stays dead because nothing ever really is.* He started back up the alley toward this white boy, then ran for him, the boy at once seeming closer but also far away.

It was past midnight when Morrison got back to his rented room with the boy. He had carried him over his shoulder for a mile before he first collapsed. The two of them lay in the weeds in the back lot of an auto body shop where the broken glass shimmered like stars fell to earth. He vomited quietly in the stale air and felt his eyes sinking and bulging in his head like a frog. The boy cast about moaning, his jeans dark from urine. Morrison hid the .38 away against the small of his back and struggled up with the dazed boy, his mouth slack and bent.

He came up through the alley by the back of his hotel, through the dry potholes and ribboned window light, past the gangway, shouldering him through the glass door propped open with a cinder block and up the two flights of stairs. He kicked open his door without using a key, laid him on the bald mattress, and opened the window. The boy thrashed about, gnashed his teeth, then slowly ground them. Morrison thought he could feel his bad dreams. Then he went down the hall with a bucket he'd been using for an ashtray.

He came back in with water and put on the fan and got it going by first spinning the blade himself. Then he turned to the boy. He was drawing breath gently through his nose. His cheeks were swollen, his eyes turning purple and black. He took off the boy's combat boots by carefully untying the laces, and looked at him, studying the face carefully, as if he could recreate the way the punches fell upon him. *I will kill whoever did this to him because you don't murder an animal, you kill it, just the way you do a gook, remember that.* He knelt beside the small bed, wet a T-shirt in the cool water, and cleaned off the boy's face, going beneath the eyes, over the upside of the jaw. The boy was still, lost in a troubled sleep. Morrison hummed, then sang, working the T-shirt over the gritty neck and throat, before his own body turned inside out from heaving and a thin line of green bile dripped from his jaw. He cupped his hand over his mouth and went on cleaning off this dark-eyed boy. *I can beat it just by looking at him. I can lose so goddamned much.*

**J**ack Tyne slept a troubled sleep and dreamed the cornfields in the country of his youth were burned by the sun down to windswept furrows. The river was a bed of cracked mud with buggy puddles that floated the leaves from the oaks and hickories on the banks. A few cornstalks remained in the dirt like withered limbs. There was no town, nothing but the dusty roads and the burned-over country. He saw everything as if through two eyes but did not once see himself.

When he woke up his head was tender and his scalp and neck hurt. He opened his swollen eyes to slits and without looking saw a fan pulling hot air through a window across some room. There was pale light on both sides of the fan, then whirring pigeons flying away and landing upon the ledge. It was dawn and he was a long way off from anywhere he knew. The room smelled of an ashtray, spilled whiskey, sweat both dry and wet. He guessed he was on a bed. He even thought he might still be dreaming but his head hurt too bad for the world of dreams.

He felt his face. There were bumps over his eyes and his cheeks had hard welts. His hand came away wet. His fingers were sprained and scraped and grit and splinters were driven up under his nails. The metal coils from the mattress springs dug into his back. He tried raising himself to his elbows, but his head went dark and he fell backward. The mattress sagged down to the floor. The room spun while he coughed up from his stomach and he broke into a cold sweat.

Put your foot on the floor, a man said.

Jack smelled a cigarette coming near to him. He looked in the direction of the voice, but his sight was blurred and grayed. The sweat chilled his skin like steel. He felt his leg being taken from the underside of his knee, then softly guided to the floor so that the bottom of his foot just touched. He rolled sideways and coughed hard, seeing through an eye corner that the mattress was bare, stained by brown fluids. A cool rag went suddenly across his mouth and he listened to it being rinsed in a bucket after each wipe. The spinning slowed, the cold sweat went away. Jack raised his head to see this man, but it was gently pushed back down as the man put the cool rag over his eyes.

Be still, he told Jack. Imagine something in your head and stare at it.

Jack imagined deer coming off the river bluffs south of Watega to stand very still and drink the brown water at twilight. The room did stop. The deer drank away.

I beat the same spinning staring at you lying here, the man said. You did not move all night, but your pulse was good. I sat in the corner and just looked at you until the sun came. I beat it like that.

His breath smelled metallic from cigarettes. There was a tired elation about his voice, as if he were relieved after surviving a disaster.

Do you know your name? the man said.

Jack Tyne.

It hurt his jaw to speak.

I'm Danny Morrison. I found you out cold last night in an alley near Damen and Grand. There was a shithead down not far from you. I'd guess you got jumped by some other niggers. Your face is bruised that way.

Son of a bitch.

You don't remember nothing, do you?

I was just walking back from work.

The rag came off his eyes long enough for the hot sunlight to sting his eyeballs beneath his lids.

There was this black guy with me, Jack said. He was all right. We were lighting cigarettes off the same match. I don't remember anything else.

I saw another guy, but I only had room for you. You don't even remember me carrying you. I'd bet that. Shit, I don't remember it myself. Last night could have been five years ago for me. I beat it. I beat it looking at you.

What did you beat? Jack asked.

Morrison said nothing for a long second.

You didn't have anything waiting for them? he said.

No.

You always got to have something ready for those assholes.

Was the other guy alive?

I only had room to carry you, Morrison said.

He was a good guy.

Fuck him, Jack Tyne. He probably set the whole thing up and the other guys got greedy.

He wasn't like that.

You don't know what kind of desperate asshole he was.

I had a room and a car and some money.

Now you got me, Morrison said.

Jack opened his eyes to slits when Morrison lifted off the rag to rinse it. He looked down at him and smiled. In the sunlight Jack saw that his face was wrecked—his nose crooked, his eyes bloodshot, his ears like cauliflower. Jack did not see this all at once because at first the whole face was just a smear and it took its mutilated form very slowly. It was like a bad burn in color. Scalded looking in the morning light.

Morrison pointed to his face.

I've been through a few doorways, he said.

Jack was embarrassed but not scared. He felt safe and he did not know why.

Morrison parted his black hair around the crown of his head as if to show Jack something.

Look at this shit, he said.

He had two bad scars, side by side. They were welted and the color of putty on his scalp and exactly the same size. Where the hair should have been, there were only the scars.

A gook sniper gave me the left one at Hue City. He just grazed it. The cocksucker got me through a hole in the wall when I thought the whole thing was over. Then I came back and my ex-father-in-law gets me on the police department and three weeks out of the academy some jazzy nigger gives me the other one. I was sitting in my squad and he gets me from between two parked cars. They look about the same, don't they?

Jack said that they did. He drew breath slowly and heard himself exhale.

You can scare a nigger dead, Morrison said. They're all talk and dope. But a gook. You got to kill a gook dead.

Jack just looked up at him.

There's a story in every mark on me, Morrison said. Even this tattoo.

He showed Jack the Marine Corps globe and anchor on his left forearm. The green ink was mottled beneath a snarl of hair.

A nigger MP gave me the stick in Oceanside the night I got it. He told me to stop drinking in the street and tried to jam me up in front of these two Mexican hookers. The girls were laughing, calling me pussy boy for letting a nigger dress me down. I called him a cocksucker and took his stick away from him and laid the asshole over the hood of a car. Broke his pretty white teeth out. I was like that back then. I thought I could take anything. But the assholes all broke their knuckles on me. Every one of them.

You were in Vietnam? Jack said.

Morrison lit a cigarette and nodded through a plume of exhaled smoke. His right ear was misshapen and curled over on itself.

My dad was at Hue City during Tet.

Was he a marine? Morrison said.

He was. But he never came home. I was a soldier five days ago. Eighty-Second Airborne.

Morrison sat alone even though Jack was there, looking out the window, down at the street. Jack thought his eyes were wet, but he did not know. The wind was blowing straight through the window faster than the fan could pull it into the room. The walls were stained from burst pipes, semen flung off the backs of hands, the ceiling made yellow from cigarette smoke. Morrison smiled, pitched the cigarette out the window, rerinsed the rag, and laid it back over Jack's eyes, the sunlight turning gauzy like dusk.

You ain't ready to look at anything, Morrison said. You just lie there and keep them closed.

In the night Jack woke from a dreamless sleep when Morrison came back into the room with ice cream and a carton of milk. The fan spun and rattled the metal cage around it. Jack lay heavy-eyed and confused while Morrison pulled the chair next to the bed. He smelled the alcohol sweat of him. Morrison opened the carton and held it so that Jack could suck the milk through a straw. His stomach rebelled; he spat up on his dirty T-shirt. Morrison wiped the milky vomit off his chin very gently, then told him to drink, and when the carton was empty, fed him vanilla ice cream with a spoon. He waited patiently between mouthfuls. It was quiet. Morrison looked upon him with love, perhaps in the way of a TV mother. Jack could hear the radio from a passing car, the frantic DJ voices jamming words into the night air. After a while Morrison stood, did a survey of the room, and dragged the chair back by the window to sit down. He was very conscious of space and never stayed close to Jack for long. He lit a cigarette, or maybe never was without one. Jack did not know because he was still seeing the room as if through holes in a fence.

I was a marine at Hue City like your old man, Morrison said. The DIs in San Diego told him what they told me on that last day of boot camp. We stood around them on the shiny barracks floor and they stood in their perfect fucking campaign hats and creased sea greens and shoes like glass. On the last day of boot camp, like you know, the DIs are a little less like gods and more like the stevedores at the stockyards. *Some of you shitbirds will not come back from Vietnam. That is no dogshit, ladies. But you will at least die marines. The commandant guarantees every one of you the same deal: a rifle, a rucksack, and a one-way ticket to Vietnam. The rest you earn. That is a fair deal because it is an honest one.* But there was nothing to earn, Jack Tyne. The DI's knew it and so did we. Who came back was like a barracks blackjack game played on a footlocker. A drawing of the cards. And a wetnose and a sharp have the same odds on a simple drawing of the cards.

I killed wounded marines at Hue City. I shot them where they lay with their guts spilled on burst concrete. I shot them in the head just like they were shit fuck gooks. I don't know if I hate myself for it. I really don't. But I do know I hate their luck.

Luck? Jack said.

I can't say that anything since has been worth the struggle. No man has been good enough to put me out of my misery.

Jack saw the sweat congealed in Morrison's two day beard when he drew his cigarette against the darkness, smoking as if the nicotine were oxygen.

I came home from Vietnam and was a cop for thirteen years, Morrison said. I worked this very street and beat assholes half to death in the alley out back. But there is nothing to beating a shithead. Sad men don't fight back. I got fucked up bad on dope, Jack Tyne. I smoked crack like a blow job hooker. I even had a real nice wife and couldn't get hard enough to screw her unless she played real dirty. I whored her. I took the light from her eyes and laughed while I did it. She started banging niggers. You know how they are with the *I love you, baby* shit. I can't even remember what she looks like. She was just there when I came home and I didn't even want her then. This clean Irish girl, the daughter of a dirty cop, her tits so white you could see the veins through the skin. I guess she didn't know how to live unless some asshole was treating her like shit. Everybody gets off on their own thing, Jack Tyne. Fuck her, fuck me. I checked into this room two years ago to die. Blow my brains out against these cum-stained walls. But I don't have the balls.

Morrison stopped talking. His story seemed to be over. He slumped in his chair and leaned it back on two legs. Jack felt the slow pumping of his pulse in his wrist and throat.

My sister has beautiful tits, Jack said. She had the body of a woman when she was still a girl and even the old men wanted to fuck her. My grandfather got nervous when she hugged him and he wouldn't let her do it after a while. He pushed her away. She started fucking my stepfather when she was fourteen and I used to watch them and she liked it. She fucked him right back and I loved looking at her tits when she did it. I got a hard-on. Sometimes I can't think about anything else. Back at Fort Bragg they beat this kid who they thought was a faggot. I thought about her tits right when they were beating him.

Morrison said nothing. He lit a cigarette and gave it to Jack. Then he looked at the wall, his eyes closed in hard sunlight.

Did you want to fuck her, Jack Tyne? he said.

Jack drew the cigarette and coughed but kept smoking. He lay on his back.

I don't know what I wanted to do, he said.

You ain't from here.

I'm from Watega County.

Did you come up here to die?

Jack was scared. He heard and said too much. He'd never listened to his own voice speak the thoughts he had about his sister. *It must be true now. It ain't like a dream anymore. I said it and heard myself and it happened.*

Did you? Morrison said.

I came up here to disappear. I tried to do it in the army, but I kept finding myself everywhere.

That's a motherfucker, ain't it?

I don't know if it is or not yet.

I bet you think I killed your old man, Morrison said.

Jack finally drew smoke without coughing.

They tell me he was an asshole, he said. He probably only would have come home from Vietnam worse than he was before.

For five days and nights they ate whatever Morrison brought in from the street: gyros with cucumber sauce wrapped in foil, hamburgers dripping catsup, cold cans of beans that Morrison opened with a P-38 can opener on his key chain. The fan spun ceaselessly even if it only spread the heat that made their necks and faces sweaty, but the air was better moving than still. They talked endlessly and each man lay bare his soul in the squalid little room above Monroe Street. Morrison sat in the chair by the window, straight-legged, never looking at Jack when he told stories that neither started nor ended. They were more like sins confessed than tales told. His face was calm and sad, his eyes lightless and sometimes closing for long seconds.

Jack sat against the wall on the thin mattress when his swollen eyes opened. Morrison's few belongings were heaped in a duffel bag by a broken sink. He'd helped Jack take his first steps and brought him to the john down the hallway, his strong arm around Jack's back, holding him up so that his feet hardly touched the bald carpet. Before that, he held an empty milk carton up for Jack to piss in. He helped him shit into a garbage bag. He wiped the heat off Jack's face with a rag and buckets full of cold water and talked about the strangeness of his new-found sobriety.

So that marine asked you to kill him? Jack said.

He did it with his eyes. The same way a woman tells you she wants to fuck you. There are certain things people cannot ask for. His guts were spilling through his fingers. It was like he was trying to hold them in.

I would have done the same thing for my buddy Wilder.

He wasn't my buddy. I didn't know him. And after that, I never wanted to know anybody.

I still would have done it.

It wasn't for him, Morrison said. It was for me. Some things are just too hard to see. He was one of them.

But you still had to see him dead.

I always will. But he was at peace. He had the look on his face like he'd gotten over on all the assholes. Sometimes I get jealous and I hate him.

But it made you do dope.

No. I liked getting high. That's what made me do dope. Even an asshole like me has to love something.

Morrison chain-smoked and pitched the butts out the window when it was his turn to hear Jack. He looked straight into his eyes. He listened with great attention, often asking Jack to repeat himself. His eyes brightened. Jack fought tears and talked for two hours, deeply moved by the way this man listened without judgment. When Jack confessed that he was a coward, another hot dusk was upon the city.

I could have gotten Donny twice, he said, maybe three

times. I could have brained him. But it wasn't like I hated the son of a bitch for fucking my sister. I was jealous that she liked it so much. She was fucking him back. Up on top of him those nights.

Morrison smiled at him and nodded, his eyes wet but not tearing. Jack Tyne sighed and soon found himself very much in love.

*He's come back from the puddles of Hue to take the dark out of the darkness and make the night just night.*

Jack Tyne went to work with Morrison delivering frozen lamb carcasses when he could walk without thinking the ground spun against the sky. It was early morning when they left the room on Monroe Street and dark, the lit buildings of the Loop rising out east like gaudy jewelry. Fat, long-winged pigeons shuttled between power line and window ledge with open beaks and strange calls. They walked the long alleys together, past the hanging iron stairs of fire escapes, past flies snarling over open dumpsters, past the pairs of emaciated dogs roaming the city behind their shadows that spooked Morrison. He carried rocks in his pockets to scare them away and he used them many times. His pockets were never without chunks of cinder blocks, broken bricks. The dogs went whining off into the morning dark and Morrison breathed easy.

They came into the market street where fat men in meat-stained aprons off-loaded quarters of cow and pig from refrigerated semitrailers. The meat steamed cold from their shoulders while they muscled it into packinghouses to hang from hooks. Men leaned against the stall doorways and sharpened butcher's knives against wet stones, their faces blank like a cat's. Forklifts raced between loading docks. Arguments raged in Spanish and Polish. The flyzappers inside the open stalls popped hysterically blue.

Jack Tyne walked proudly beside Morrison in his borrowed blue jeans and a T-shirt with cut-off sleeves. He thought them men of analogous blood. Through the corners of his eyes he saw Morrison watching over him while the ex-cop walked lean-hipped, shod in heavy boots. The smell of thawing meat was everywhere.

Morrison pulled a cigarette from his pocket and raised a match. He pointed up the long street of stalls to the one at the very end near Halsted and the idling semi trucks. Out front, there were two Mexicans loading lamb carcasses into the back of a van. They had unsmiling faces and worked very fast. Morrison spoke before exhaling his smoke.

That's where we work, he said. That's the van. I drive, and you run the lambs in.

It doesn't seem like anything.

The worst part is cleaning up the blood after they've half thawed. The cats will be thick around here. All fighting to get inside the van and lick up that blood. You just shoot the hose at them, but some don't even care about getting wet. They want the blood real bad. You'll see.

Jack walked, listening.

You don't mind that for six bucks an hour.

I was making eight as a mover, Jack said.

Tough shit.

Morrison grinned around his cigarette, then put his arm around Jack and held him close for a long second while they walked and laughed.

The stall was the size of a big garage with an office in a loft above the freezer doorway. The metal door was rolled open. The fat Greek stood at the bottom of the stairs and smoked and drank coffee in the way of a man who had not been to sleep. His white loafers were scuffed with black marks, cigarette ash spotted his wrinkled silk shirt. The Mexicans brought the lamb carcasses out of the freezer with gloved hands and the skin smoked cold. It was red and white because the blood of their withers was still frozen hard. The lambs all had blue eyes that were strangely attached to the sockets. Their necks wiggled while the Mexicans loaded them in the back of the van on a sheet of cardboard. Stacked there in the dark, the skinned and gutted lambs looked like toothy prehistoric birds.

You think you could get drunk enough to kiss one of these? Morrison said.

I almost messed with a whore uglier than them when I was sober, Jack said.

A hard dick always points north, don't it? Morrison said.

I didn't touch her.

Your asshole buddy got the one you wanted.

How did you know?

There's always an asshole buddy, and you ain't a fighter.

Jack Tyne spat and stood listening, vaguely thinking of Keller and his game-show-host smile and wondering if he was in line for the third stripe yet. Morrison walked into the stall and talked to the Greek. The big exhaust fan near the roof was sucking the air straight out of the stall. The Greek did not look at Jack very long if at all.

He watched the Mexicans work in the silent manner of running rivers, gusting wind, when a sweaty black came up the street pushing a grocery cart stacked high with wooden pallets. The black dodged trucks and fork-lifts and lines of workmen unloading quartered beef. He was tailed by mangy dogs who rushed forward and fought to sniff his wrecked shoes. His face seemed made of hard mud, his head curlicues of gray. The man pushed his cart up to Jack and eyed him while the dogs reared and growled at each other, their yellow teeth slick with drool. The pallets on the cart teetered and the man steadied them with his shoulder.

Last night, he said to Jack, the motherfuckers beat me until I almost shit. I just wish I could fly. You know. Fly off and away.

Who beat you? Jack said.

The motherfuckers beat me. Who else?

The man stank like the water at the bottom of a dump-ster. He bore no marks of violence except those from age.

I ain't the kind of man to look at sin, he said. There ain't no future in it. I just wish I could fly but the Lord set me to walking. All his children get shoes for walking when they need wings for flying. But there ain't no nigger angels, anyway. No man's painted one. But they there. The painting man just didn't see them. You know why?

No, Jack said.

The man's eye whites had gone red. The dogs whined and scratched at the pavement with their scant backsides and then ran off with their shadows.

They fly way too fast, he said. Just like you should. Danny Irish is a wild man. He ain't like the rest of us.

Jack turned away and watched the Mexicans load the last of the lambs. The blue eyeballs peered many ways out of the van. The Mexicans curved their mouths into dark grins and wiped their hands on stained aprons.

Crazy, they said of Morrison. Just fucking nuts.

**T**hey crossed and recrossed through the North Side of the city countless times in the next days, past the lightless marquees of dollar movie houses, taverns without windows where beer signs swung in the wind, the gum-stained sidewalks outside El stations where crippled men sold socks twined off in bunches. The crowded streets took them butcher shop by butcher shop, storefronts fixed between resale shops and Indian video stores, where dark-eyed Greeks worked in hot back rooms and the sweat from their unshaven faces fell upon tables strewn with ribbons of sliced flesh. Their humor was dark like their mustaches, these men whose living it was to chop meat. When they saw that Morrison's boy was new to the route, even squeamish about the lambs he delivered, they put their lunatic eyes into Jack's own and winked slowly, as if advertising hookers, before severing a lamb's head with one clean swipe of their cleaver. The rended heads wobbled by their bloody tennis shoes but never rolled, even nodding on the concrete floors as if laughing big laughs with the butchers. Some were excellent ventriloquists and threw their voices so that the cleaved heads greeted Jack in broken English, offering free fellatio, while the butchers sharpened long knives against whetstones and tested the blades' sharpness by shaving off patches of black arm hair. There were butchers who were missing fingers altogether, and they waved their stumps at Jack with mock coyness, even blowing him kisses and asking him if he liked it Greek.

Morrison watched Jack keep his eyes to himself and work quietly as if he were anywhere but the butcher shops. He was a strong boy, carrying a frozen carcass over each shoulder from the van into these butcher shops where the flies thumped against the screen doors like hail. He hung them head down from hooks by the metal wire banding together their legs, and in the heat they were quick to thaw. But Morrison could see that Jack was shaken by all of it. His eyes blinked like camera shutters. He winced after each cleaver stroke as if he were losing his own head and hind. He looked out the back doors the way people stare into wind, hoping to find somewhere to put his eyes.

At the end of these days, they drove back to the men of the market who sat shoulder to shoulder on car hoods and drank beer. Sallow haze at dusk. The full-blown games of grab-ass, the fistfights over filched bets put off since noon. Cops in their cruisers with hawkish faces and dead eyes that gouged the city dark open like a bayonet. Jack scrubbed the liquefied fat and blood from the van floor with Ajax and a green pad like a penitent barracks thief on extra duty while the Mexicans hosed down the stall and swept the water into the drains. Morrison stood smoking, as was his habit, loving the way this boy from the cornfields worked silently without ever questioning why it was him cleaning the blood and not somebody else. He was a good soldier. The ex-cop could see it.

Jack was sitting in the back of the van with his legs straight before him. He was wet from the wash water, his pants stained white from Ajax, his palm to his nose. Morrison smoked with one boot propped on the bumper hitch, watching the cats snarl and hiss for dips on the blood-soaked cardboard sheet they used to line the van floor. Jack looked at him.

How do you get the smell of lamb off your hands? Jack said.

Morrison laughed and looked at the grit lining the boy's lips.

You don't, he said. You learn to live with it.

Jack only nodded. The van was perfectly scoured, glinting wet.

You ever think about going after that stepfather of yours? Morrison said.

I'm never going down there again, Jack said. There ain't nothing to see.

You went down there before.

It was a mistake. I was looking for home, but there really isn't such a place.

Morrison looked at the water stains running up the legs of Jack's blue jeans and then at his terrified eyes.

*I'll get that fat son of a bitch for him. He doesn't have to be so goddamned scared. There's no reason at all because the only thing we have to lose is what we are looking at right now. He needs to know that.*

They sat one night in Morrison's rented room in two chairs by the open window and spread potted meat on saltine crackers, eating mustard sardines from tins with their fingers. The cool had come that morning when the black clouds wound over the horizon where the sky met the rim of Lake Michigan. There was no wind, so the clouds took all afternoon to hood the city. Morrison twisted the cap off a Budweiser quart and split it in two coffee cups while the first rain came in three months, a soft summer rain falling slant through the streetlights.

The scabs upon Jack's face had peeled and become small. The bruises beneath his eyes had faded from yellow black to the color of flesh. He lost his soldier's haircut and the hair sprouted wildly on his neck. The rain quickened and darkened the concrete like the sky and the webbed dust in the gutters turned to mud. Morrison was afraid that the boy would go now that he was well, disappear from his life like the closing and opening of eyes. That was too much to think about right now. The boy ruined things. If he left, Morrison would never be alone again, only lonely.

He turned holding the cup of beer and in turning saw Jack's haunted eyes and the sadness that lived in their gaze. In the first lightning flare the city seemed a thing pulled from a magician's hat and then put back inside again.

You ever think about asking your old man anything? Morrison said.

Jack looked at him and then looked back out the window when the thunder sounded three times.

I used to have these daydreams that he'd come from the dead, Jack said. He'd sit by me and tell me what I needed to know. How to be a man. How to fight. He even told me how everything was going to end up. Things would be set right, he'd say. They have to be. But it wasn't really him I was dreaming about. He was some guy I saw on TV. That's all I ever had to go on about having a father. Shit. I'd even make up memories I had of him when I never even had any.

It's better that you didn't, Morrison said. The one thing that ruins having an old man is having one.

I was lucky that way. I had the kind you make up.

That isn't so bad.

It is when you go making up everything else about your life.

Jack sat holding the cup tightly. He looked out the window at the light bleeding on the wet streets beneath them and at the sky above jumping and rolling from lightning. His eyes became wet, then thin tears came.

My old man was a waste, Morrison said. He'd drink aftershave lotion if that's all he could find. This little Irish motherfucker who could get his ass whipped by a big tomcat. But I gave up hating him a long time ago.

Why's that? Jack said.

Every man is a little fucked up about something he didn't get, Morrison said. A father ain't no different than you or me that way.

Morrison refilled the coffee cups and set the empty bottle on the floor.

You know I was ready to kill myself before I found you, he said. I wanted to more than anything. I had dreams about kissing silence. Ramming my tongue down its throat like silence was a broad. But now I don't want it. And I can't tell you why.

I bet you thought you were already dead, Jack said.

Something like that. But I don't know why I think I'm so alive right now.

Jack's lips trembled when he smiled.

You've never thought about getting revenge against Donny? Morrison said.

Lots of times. But I don't care anymore.

Morrison pushed back in his chair and watched Jack sit as if he were on a horse, staring coldly at nothing the way he might regard burnt, grassless country with long skies and rugged mountains heaped upon the horizon.

When you pretended your old man was talking to you, Morrison said, did you ever ask him what you should do about Donny?

I never brought it up to him.

What did you ask him? Morrison said.

I just let him tell me things. Like the way you do. But if
I could ask him anything, I'd want to know if he was ever
happy.

That's it?

I can't think of anything else I'd really want to know.

Jack said nothing more. His distant eyes turned afraid,
even pitiful. He was no more a soldier than a sick cat. Morrison let it drop and they lit cigarettes and smoked quietly
while the real rain came in black sheets that wafted and
rolled from the wind off the lake. Morrison knew this rain
would fall for many days and flood the sewers, and by day-
break the refugee rats would be playing on the alley bricks
like children.

The rain blew slantwise through the door that went into
the Greek's stall when Morrison opened it for Jack. There
were four waiters playing cards around a square table, old
men with gray hair sprouting from their ears. The mongoloid boy with crooked eyes filled their glasses from a
Scotch bottle. He drooled and moved in a wandering way
and every drink he poured confused him as if each glassful
were his first time doing it. He held the bottle hard by the
neck and thought for long seconds about whether to bring
the glass up to the bottle or the bottle down to the glass.
The waiters slouched in their blue restaurant uniforms
with name tags on the lapels and anted with twenty-dollar
bills after sorting the cards in their hands. A space heater
warmed their legs.

Morrison left Jack by the door and he sat down on a
stack of packing pallets, careful not to see anything that
might look back, his worried eyes peering straight across
the room at the brick wall where mops and brooms were
propped in buckets.

I got to find out what he wants us to do, he said.

Jack nodded with the gnome face of a child.

The stall ran up to a staircase in the back of a large room
where the Greek's office perched over the meat locker.

Smoke rose from the mouths of the waiters as it did from the ashtrays. The mongoloid had run out of Scotch and he stood gape-mouthed, looking down into the bottle to make sure. His shirt pocket was full of dollar tips the waiters had shoved into it. His tongue hung from his mouth, dirty and white like river foam, while he held the bottle up to the light and shook it by the neck.

The office door opened and the Greek came heavily down the stairs. He stood on the bottom step and wiped his eyes and yawned. His gut kept untucking his blue silk shirt and he had long stopped trying to shove it back inside his pants.

Well, Danny Irish, he said.

Morrison nodded, coming up the steps.

They stood together looking out over the stall as if it were wide open country. The Greek smiled without humor while Morrison gave him the delivery receipts bound to a clipboard. The fall wind was blowing through the deserted market street and driving the rain in tiny squalls against the door of the loading bay. They could hear the drops hitting the metal all the way across the room.

I need you to collect some debts, the Greek said.

I don't do that anymore, Morrison said. I told you.

You'd rather deliver dead lambs in the rain for six dollars an hour? the Greek said. I think you will change your mind. You are not fit to work.

I make the deliveries.

The Greek put two fingers to his mouth and drug the cigarette between them. He stood one step above Morrison.

No, Danny Irish, he said. You are not here to do the work of Mexicans and I think you know this. You are much too desperate.

I don't know what the hell you're talking about.

You scare men with the ghosts that haunt you, the Greek said. That is what you do. It is your card.

I don't scare you.

I own parts of you like I do these gambling waiters. Without me, none of you could be who you are. But then, part of you and them also own me. Our needs and talents have married us. I think you know this.

I don't drug anymore. Not since the boy came around.

So you have a wife in that boy?

It ain't like that.

The Greek stepped off the last step. His shirt was open at the neck, his cigarette between his fingers like a diamond ring. He peered across the stall at Jack standing by the door looking out the window.

You scare your boy, he said.

No.

But he is already scared. He uses you not to be afraid. I see it in his eyes, the way he never looks at a thing that might look back. Then one day you will be who you are, Danny Irish. He will go and you will have nothing again.

That ain't going to happen.

Everything happens. Always. So I will wait for you to have nothing, then you will find my money.

The Greek laughed through his swollen nose. The mongoloid boy was still circling the table of gamblers with the empty bottle raised to his crossed eyes. He stared through the clear glass as if it had been full of Scotch the last time he looked. Drool seeped from his mouth. He truly wanted to know where the whiskey had gone. The waiters took their cards from the dealer with faces cold like the concrete floor. Morrison wished that Jack would turn from the door and look at him, maybe smile as a son might, but he did not, and instead put his eyes closer to the window. The Greek came off the last step and leaned against the freezer door, sighing as if to mock Morrison.

You are moony, he said.

I just worry about him. He doesn't have anybody.

The boy will go back home. He will choose life. He is still young.

No.

The Greek put two fingers to his lips to caution silence.

Some men build crosses, he said. Other men hang on them. While still others nail men to the wood and watch them die. We both know who we are.

You talk too much shit.

You hang; I watch you wait to die.

Fuck you.

The Greek was mimicking the way Morrison mooned over Jack, feigning a look of gentleness with his dark eyes, when the ex-cop swung against his sleek, oiled head. The fat man's face turned from the force of the punch while blood sprayed from his mouth like vomit. Then Morrison belted him three times in the throat. The Greek's eyes rolled up under his eyelids though they did not close. His knees gave way before he collapsed on the concrete floor. He tried sitting up against the freezer door, but Morrison screamed and kicked his face until he fell sideways and made no effort to protect himself. His hairy gut spilled from his shirttail. Morrison smiled and circled, perhaps a dog from his dreams, yellow-toothed, froth leaking over his thin lips. He kicked the Greek until the sight of his white gut gyrating made him laugh hysterically.

**J**ack crouched by the door of the stall where the rain strafed against the small window and smeared the streetlight in the glass. He was afraid to move. Morrison's face was wet and dirty from the rain, his eyes flat and lightless in a way Jack had never known eyes to be. He circled the Greek and panted. The fat man lay awkwardly on folded legs, his mouth blood wet. Then Morrison started howling and kicked against his ribs while he tried rising to his elbows. Soon the Greek stopped moving. The mongoloid dropped the Scotch bottle on the floor, gawking through bouncing eyes, his tongue slipped from his mouth like the Greek's. The waiters at the card game were up from the table and grabbing their bills from the green felt and running past Jack for the door with crooked toupees and open shirts, filing one by one out into the rain. They left their coats over the chair backs and their cards strewn on the floor with the broken glass.

The mongoloid mimicked Morrison's dark laughter. He looked back at Jack and grinned like a cartoon character until his eyes closed. With his dwarfed legs, he imitated Morrison's kicks against the table leg until it tipped over and broke the glasses that still floated ice cubes. The ex-cop was like a dog turned feral, strangely alive, his violence almost a beautiful dance. The Greek was a heap of fat and drool and black hair. The mongoloid jumped up and down, his ass almost touching his heels each time he landed. Jack was halfway out the door, watching the slowest of the waiters splash along the flooded potholes, when Morrison turned his head carefully and looked at him from across the room. His eyes were hollow and dark where cyanic blue once was, eyes that had seen and brought death and begged Jack into their colors.

Jack went running out into the rain and the wet streets, moon-white with streetlight. Shriveled hookers slumped in marketstall doorways smiled with open mouths and flashed him stretched breasts. He ran with a half-pint of Scotch that Morrison had jammed into his belt, heading north for the metal rush of the Lake Street El, the car lights strafing the buildings like soundless gunfire. Ahead, he saw a place where the street was torn up. The asphalt had been burst with a jackhammer and was heaped in a pile around the hole. He went to his knees behind it and listened for bootfalls but heard nothing but the rain once the El train passed. He kept trying to forget Morrison's eyes, but there was nothing he could think to do it. *My father would have had them if he lived. The same dark holes like he was dead without his body even knowing it.*

He came up the rail line beyond Green Street past pigeons dead in the gutter flow. The tracks went straight across the muddy river into the Loop. A fog came over the city from the east and the great skyscrapers were only blurs of light as if fires beneath the sea. He waded through the dark water flooding the rails until he thought he was lost enough in the fog. He walked over to a concrete wall right off the tracks and hid, crouching among some scrub trees. He had to go somewhere, run off into the wet city blocks away from those eyes, but he did not move. From time to time he drank from the half-pint in slow sips and looked off across the network of tracks, remembering the joyless barracks parties and the cheap bourbon chased back with cans of Coke.

The water beyond the green track lights splashed as if a man had fallen down. Then came the obscene sounds of shoes sucking in the mud. Jack looked. The fog settled low on both sides of the rail line. He looked again. By the switchtrack, a man was coming to his knees and cursing the Mother of Jesus in a hillbilly accent, yelling like he was the last person in a world turned to dark water. He stood and his arms hung limp before he wiped the mud off his bearded face and flung it back in the water. Jack was motionless in the scrub trees. The man scanned the concrete wall like a paranoid before fixing his eyes on Jack's boots. He waded closer and squinted. He was very thin and his long hair hung in his face, his surplus field jacket open like his mouth.

That someone? he said.

Jack was quiet for a long second. Yes, he said.

The man waded closer. He stood in the water past his knees and eyed Jack with the unmannered intensity of an idiot.

You the guard? he said. I've seen a lot of guards around here. Mostly niggers.

No, Jack said. I'm nobody like that.

I ain't seen so many niggers in such high places until I come to Chicago.

Jack said nothing.

And yin's? the man said.

Jack stared at this skinny, violent-looking man.

And yin's? Have you ever seen so many boss niggers?

No.

They watched the water scuttle from the wind. The man took a half-smoked cigarette from behind his ear. It was soaked. Across his knuckles was tattooed the word LOVE.

You ain't got a light, do you? he said.

My matches are all wet.

Shit, the man said. It'd be nice to get a light for this butt. You sure them matches ain't no good?

I tripped in the water the same as you did, Jack said.

Son of a bitch. You saw me bust my ass? A nigger would have cut me when I was down. Good thing you ain't a nigger.

Yes, Jack said.

Where you headed? the man said.

Nowhere.

I'm going to California to pick fruit. I hear they make a white man boss over the Mexicans. You just show up and you got men under you. I've been waiting around here all day for a train slow enough to jump.

There aren't any freights that pass through here, Jack said. It's only commuter trains and Amtrak.

I hitched up here from Knoxville a few days ago, the man said. Everybody along the way told me I could get a freight out of Chicago. I just figured if I waited around here long enough, one would pass through. But this nigger guard down there started mouthing me. A white man can't take no sass off a nigger and feel one bit good about himself. Them Mexicans out there in California better do right what I tell them.

Jack looked at him and his baggy work pants bunched about his legs.

Those little trains sure move through here, the man said. I bet people get killed all the time. I'd even bet that some of them was even kids sparking in a car.

Maybe, Jack said.

I bet the boy was about to shoot, the man said. Wouldn't
that be some shit. Them fucking like monkeys and then
wham.

It would.

You better believe it would. There was a crazy man
back home who roamed mountain roads and was murder-
ing all the people who were parked and fucking. He'd wait
for Haas to dump his load and then he'd gun him in the
head.

The man smiled crooked teeth at Jack and made a pistol with his finger.

Pow, pow, he said. Then one night he comes across two
faggots ass-fucking and the gun jams. Guess what happened to that crazy son of a bitch?

What? Jack said.

The two faggots plain-ass whipped him. You'd never
think it but two faggots is two men and I bet some of them
can be pretty mean. Is that whiskey over there?

The man took the half-pint from Jack's hand and uncapped it before slugging the Scotch hard. He drank half
the bottle.

That done it, he said. I just love to feel that burn.

Jack took back the bottle. The man's eyes were like
searchlights upon him. He smelled of rotten food.

Ain't this one hell of a place to spend the night, he said.

It is, Jack said. Have a good one.

Jack sank to his ankles in the mud when he jumped
down off the wall. He stared across the tracks in the yellow
fog.

Hey, the man said. You don't got a couple bucks you
could loan me. I'll take your address and send it on directly
from California.

I don't have it, Jack said.

The man followed him, making noise in the water.

I ain't ate nothing since that trucker fed me, he said. It's
been two days.

Jack kept walking. I don't have anything, he said.

I think you're a lying sack of shit, the man said. You had enough to buy that fancy fuck whiskey.

Jack eyed him over his shoulder. The man was wading fast and looking serious, muttering son of a bitch under his breath.

I'd like to see what's in that back pocket of yours, he said. That's something I'd like to see. You goddamned piss-willie. Leave a white man hungry.

Jack moved faster, high-stepping in the water, his boots weighted with mud.

I see that fucking wallet from here, the man said.

The rails glowed silver in the murky water while Jack waded toward the boom of traffic on Milwaukee Avenue. He held the bottle as if it were a grenade. He was almost across the second set of tracks when the man jumped him from behind and they went into the water together. The man was trying to swing at him, wild punches with bony fists. Jack kneed him in the groin. The man quit swinging and tried biting his nose, but Jack reared on his back leg and swung the bottle against his head. The glass broke in his hand. The man's forehead opened grimly before his eyes rolled up and he fell backward, the muddy water splashing around him.

Jack stood and ran down the tracks into the fog. His hand bled. The taste of foamy spit was in his mouth. The water was still. The distant sound of an Amtrak whistling out of Union Station came drifting up the tracks. The man lay in the water where he had fallen. Jack pushed his hand in his pocket where it pulsed and bled and ran back to Green Street the exact way he had first come. He yelled out into the fog for Morrison.

**M**orrison's foot was raised to stomp the Greek's throat where he lay cold on the floor of the stall and curled against two plastic garbage cans. He was no longer trying to defend himself. His split nose gushed blood. His chest heaved from breath. The mongoloid was kicking the stacked pallet where Jack had sat, his laughter like the yelps of kenneled dogs. Morrison looked at his twisted mouth and stopped himself from caving the Greek's neck and went running out into the rain after Jack. He did not know if the boy had been gone an hour or a minute or why he was kicking the Greek. He just woke up and there he was. The mongoloid was running around the street behind him, the puddles exploding beneath his footfalls, a pale vapor surging from his mouth. *I have done so many bad things, but God bring me back this boy.*

He ran down past the row of Greek restaurants on Halsted and they were all closed. Behind the long windows, the waiters stacked chairs on the tables and swept bread crusts and cigarette butts off the floor. A lonely street of empty bus stops and parked cars, grayish water running in the gutters and streaming down the sewer grates. Morrison went inside the bus station on Harrison, wet from the night, running along the gouged wooden benches and looking into the eyes of greasy men who looked back as if corpses and waited for all things except a bus. He checked the piss-marred men's room, the tiny stalls without doors, the mirror cracked into spider webs. He left and roamed the fog and the weedy mud of back lots and then down by the river where the dark eddy water went swirling around concrete piers. Many times he thought he saw Jack's lank figure coming toward him in the dark, but it was only rags of fog billowing through the shadows, coursing the outer dark beyond the hooped streetlight. Sometimes it was a couple of whores reeling off among the potholes on broken heels while they wiped the semen off their faces with paper bags and adjusted their wigs.

At his hotel stoop he found the paddy wagon parked across the street by a vacant lot. Inside, the flex-cuffed drunks flapped on the bench seats like strung fish and gnashed their teeth in the dark. The rain became a small drizzle that leaned through the streetlights. Morrison sat on the steps and smoked while two tired cops drug a drunk out of the weeds. The fog was strobed blue by the spinning lights of the wagon. The cops moved as methodically as marionettes and pulled a drenched wino through the mud and the gravel. His head swayed and his neck bent as if in prayer.

The drunks screamed and called the people of the world cocksuckers when the cops opened the wagon. A black sat by the door with swollen eyes and rested his head back against the wall, his nose dripping blood. One bloated drunk stuck out his head to see and the slag-eyed cop popped him in the solar plexus with the slapstick. The man fell hard and backwards to the floor where a shackled speed freak was lifting his bound legs and stomping. The cops picked the wino up like a battering ram and shoved him inside without watching themselves. The paddy wagon soon sped off into the fog and turned the corner so fast that the men would rattle off the walls. Morrison knew this game well and he also knew that the roundup would continue until dawn and when day broke and the fog lifted there would still be many drunks the cops had missed.

He pitched his cigarette in the street when a figure came running along a row of parked cars, veiled by the fog, until it was within twenty feet of him. It stood watching. He could hear the steady drawing of breath and even the sound of crying somewhat more faintly. He looked away and looked back. It was his boy, soaked like driftwood, mud clotting his short hair. He trembled and eyed Morrison in the way of a scared dog. He did not speak. He stood there staring at him and crying. His hand was cut and dark with blood and it held a broken piece of bottle glass. Morrison walked over and put his arms around Jack and the boy did not hug him back. They stood a long time like that in the rain and never said a word.

The weather did not change. The days were cold and very wet with grayish water flowing in the gutters. Morrison found them work gutting the apartments in three-flats on the North Side of the city for rehab into condominiums. The man who contracted them was not much older than Jack and wore a suit and had fine teeth and never looked into their eyes when he spoke to them. The first day they rose early and beat the plaster from the wall studs with sledges until their hands blistered and bled and the hammer handles tore the skin off their palms. They smashed the stools from bathroom floors and made the old mildewed tubs rubble and tore down whole walls and pried off cabinets with crow bars. Jack wrapped his bloody hands in gauze and wore gloves but the blood soaked through by noon and made them wet as dishrags. Morrison wielded the hammer like a man possessed and his bloody palms never seemed to bother him. He gasped and panted while he burst the porcelain and plaster alike, his sad eyes looking upon the apartments as if they were scenes from old nightmares. From time to time he looked desolately over at Jack and forced a smile and laughed to himself. Jack kept his distance and worked. *I'm somebody else to him. He never sees me even when he is looking at me. I'm a dead man he's trying to make alive again, maybe even turning me into himself in a way he never was.*

It was almost dark and raining lightly and they were wet and their faces were wet in the white light from the hang lamp powered by a long orange drop cord. With coal shovels they scooped up the rubble and pitched it from the second-story back door into a dumpster left in the alley. The burst plaster fell upon the cracked wall studs and floor slats, sounding like an avalanche. When they were done, they leaned the shovels against the gutted walls, their handles blood-smeared, then huddled forward in the apartment by a space heater. Morrison smiled like a somber young boy and offered Jack a cigarette. His dim reflection was in the window glass and through it the drops fell slantwise and slow and sliced his face like thin razors. Nothing was ever said about the beating of the Greek or the way Jack ran off into the rain. Jack smoked and held his marred hands against the orange heating element, scared by Morrison's reflection, as if in it were some darker self more true in aspect than the sad eyes that looked upon him. All Jack needed was two more weeks of working and he'd have the bus fare to go see Wilder in Virginia, and this strange man Morrison would be nothing more than a story told over beers and shots.

Morrison smoked and scratched a spot just above his ear.

I wonder if your old man ever felt like a god in Vietnam? he said.

I don't know what you mean, Jack said.

That was the best part of it, Morrison said. You could be a raggedy-assed nigger or hillbilly over there and you could do anything to the gooks you wanted. You could buy whole families of them to wash your ass and suck your dick and for enough money, they'd cup their hands so you could shit in them. If one pissed you off, you just shot him, burned his hovel down, killed his pigs and chickens, fucked his daughter in the ass. It didn't matter. The officers didn't care because we were giving them dead gooks to count. The company commanders had contests over body counts like kids collecting those soup labels for school. They made their careers on dead gooks.

One time I was up in this chopper over the Perfume River and all these little gooks were floating along in their sampans. Some had motors. Some had oars. Whole gook families lived on these things just like dink river trash. The door gunner was this big nigger with a lazy eye and he had no use for gooks. He said his buddy got killed in a Da Nang whorehouse. The guy was getting his dick sucked when two gook cowboys ran in and cut his throat for forty-six bucks. We were flying above the river and he points to a box full of ten-pound rocks and yells to me over the rotor wash that he and the pilot have a game they play and would I like to try. He said they sink sampans with rocks. They just hover over and drop the fuckers. All those gooks in those fucked-up boats are running guns for the VC anyway, he said. I told him he was full of bullshit. No rock could sink a boat. So he hooked me up in the harness and the pilot started to hover over a sampan heading our way. He gave me a rock and I leaned out and dropped the son of a bitch and the rock went right through the sampan and it sank. The little dinks were swimming around in the shit brown water and jabbering gook at me. The door gunner just smiled all toothy and handed me another rock. There were a lot more sampans and this guy had a rock for every one of them.

Was everybody like that? Jack said.

After they saw some dead Americans they were. It was like being a white cop in a ghetto over there. But your old man probably made more gooks VC than the VC did. Us Marines were like that. Funny thing is, I ain't sorry about it. I used to be sorry about not being sorry, but fuck them. The dead are lucky. We're just the wounded. We drew the shit card.

I really wouldn't know what to say about my father, Jack said.

The shadows of the rain falling through the streetlight dotted and rolled on the long wooden bar. Jack and Morrison sat close together on two stools by the wall. Out in the street the rain squalled through the darkness and blurred the passing headlights of semis pulling out from the truck lots on Monroe Street. Wet firemen from the Greek Town house drank beer from glasses and whiskey shooters and threw darts wildly that hit the wall, the window, the high-backed stools around the empty tables across the room. *It was last winter when Quinn's eyes froze in his sockets like fucking ice cubes in a tray. Do you remember that night? That fire in that shit woodframe down at 55th and the Ryan. Those fucking animals down there. Quinn getting retired because some shithead bought Chivas Regal instead of paying the gas bill and turned the bathtub into a firepit to keep the hawk out of his asshole. Goddamn those shitheads.* They laughed like barking dogs and staggered heavily to the wall where they bent over to pick up their darts. The buttons on their blue uniforms gapped. Their shirttails came untucked from their waists. *Throw darts at my ass you cocksucker and I'll put icy hot in your shorts.*

In the red bar light and drifting smoke, Morrison eyed the scene balefully and drank the bottom from his beer glass without swallowing, then nodded as if to convince himself of something. He wiped his mouth with his field jacket sleeve before slapping Jack on the shoulder. Jack looked at him and forced a smile and then looked at his mutilated palms. Morrison lifted his hand at the bartender and gestured at his empty glass with two fingers. The bartender squinted at him through the smoke with small rat's eyes and held up a beer glass dripping with rinse water. He wore a faded denim shirt and most of the buttons had been replaced with safety pins or not at all. Morrison nodded.

That's what I want, asshole, he said under his breath.

The old man across the room banged his empty highball glass on the counter. He sat where the bar curved into the wall and glared at the bartender with a cold cigarette butt in his mouth. The ice cubes jumped from the glass and landed on the floor. His coal eyeballs were motionless behind slit lids and half hidden away in the deep pleats of his face. The bartender filled Morrison's draught and waved the old man away with his hand. The old man's lips trembled and he banged the glass harder and jabbered the way deaf people speak. Jack turned away from him and watched the firemen's darts hit the wall.

The bartender rolled his eyes when he set the beer down because the old man had become louder, pounding the glass like a gavel to call this world to order.

The old prick's started early, he said.

Morrison shook his head and drank the beer.

Go easy, Jimmy, he said.

Jimmy laughed through his nose while he sipped off a drink he kept hidden beneath the bar. His eyes ran from the smoke. He had just shaved before his shift and there were fresh shaving cuts on his neck.

Fuck off, Danny Irish, he said. You can get your ass up and leave anytime. But not me. I got to look all night at this old motherfucker while he tries to talk his bullshit. The bastard smells. He doesn't even wash his teeth.

You can't smell dirty teeth, Morrison said.

No. But you got to see them. You ever look at something like him for eight hours? There ain't no future in it.

You're not real soft on the eyes, Morrison said.

Go kiss him, then, Jimmy said.

The bartender held the cigarette to his lips even after he drew it.

Last week the old fuck tried to kill himself, he said. But I didn't get that lucky. He started his niece's car in her garage down on Emerald but a window was busted so all the exhaust got out. All he did was faint and piss himself. But his niece has some nice tits. She comes in after him sometimes but never sticks around. A perfect fucking D-cup.

The old man eyed Jack and made him nervous. His cheeks were yellow like the cracked ceiling and sagged with wrinkles. He pointed to his glass and tried talking. One side of his face was very still as if he'd had a stroke. The spilled ice cubes made small puddles on the bar.

Who found him? Jack said.

The whole fucking neighborhood, Jimmy said. The old prick fell against the horn while he was pissing like a racehorse. The old broads were running around crossing themselves.

Morrison's lips curved a sad grin as he watched himself drink his beer in the bar-back mirror. Jimmy smirked at the old man and emptied all of the ashtrays into one.

Don't go crying on me, he said to Morrison. I think you Irish bastards would rather cry than fuck.

Morrison looked vaguely away from his own image.

You don't get it, he said. That old man is Patrick Hoey. I knew him when I was a kid and he was a drunk then. He was a nose-gunner on a B-17 and he used to tell us about riding whole missions with shit in his flight suit because he was so scared. He flew over Germany like that for two years, always in his own shit. He saw Americans parachuting on fire from the sky after the flak gutted their planes. Men looking right into his eyes while they passed by the nose and him knowing they were going to burn a while before they died. There was nothing to do but turn his guns on them. I don't think he's ever thought about anything else.

If you like him so much, Jimmy said, then take the old bastard home and let him fuck your sister. I'm sick of looking at him. He don't even wash himself.

The old man held his glass out and smacked his toothless gums. He gestured cruelly with his bony hand, his face spectral in the red bar light. He eyed Jack hard and Jack could see that in his day, he was a tough guy whom other men did not ignore, perhaps like Morrison. But now he was a filthy old man. Finally, Jack turned his stool away to face the wall.

Morrison ground his cigarette in a clean ashtray and pushed a ten-dollar bill toward the well.

Let him drink this up, he said.

He gulps his drinks, Jimmy said. He'll be begging for more in twenty minutes. There ain't no end to it.

Pour him one, Morrison said.

Jimmy looked at the money and then at the old man.

You might be buying, he said. But I ain't selling.

The old man was pointing at the money from across the bar when Jimmy walked over to him. His skin hung in folds off his face. No more, Jack heard the bartender say. He repeated himself and used his hands to talk. The old man put his hands on the bar to brace himself, then stood, his knees forever bent, before stumbling. His face scowled while he reeled and found balance. His arms were like an insect's legs, quivering inside his coat sleeves. There was a pride in his bearing. He looked around for a man to return his stare the way a kid might pick a fight without saying a word, but the few drinkers at the bar were already lost in beer glasses and their own booze laughter. He staggered straight and slow to the door and went out into the rain.

Morrison looked at Jimmy, his face like a gas-can lid.

He would have drank and went home, he said. He just wanted to be around men.

You don't know how shitty he gets when the money runs out, Jimmy said.

I would have paid.

Not tonight. I don't want to go to sleep thinking about his teeth.

You don't get it, Morrison said. He has these stories to tell and nobody knows how to hear them. You don't know what it's like.

It was raining hard outside the barred tavern windows. The dirty fog that blew in wet gusts half-concealed the old man while he crossed and recrossed the street many times. His pant legs blew against his gaunt limbs and he high-stepped along the flooded gutter. Jack watched cars pass him in the fog, the unseen drivers sounding their horns. The old man did not seem to care. Jack guessed that the old man tried suicide on a night like this. The weather probably got into his knees and elbows and the pain drove him to it.

Jimmy poured Morrison a double shot of J&B. The ex-cop looked into the glass for a long time before drinking it with a swallow.

That bastard talks crazy about things, Jimmy said. You ain't never heard him. He can't hardly talk, but he tells you stories anyway. If you walk away, he only yells. Last night he starts in about his time in a German POW camp. He says that the Nazi guards would beat the Russian prisoners with clubs where they lived like rats and lice in a compound all of their own. A man and a dog can sound the same way when they're being beaten, he says. It got so bad with them Russians howling that nobody could tell them apart from dogs. He got all afraid of himself because he didn't know the difference. He then tells me that he'd lie in the barracks and dream that someday he wouldn't have ears to hear the world. I said no ears. What kind of shit is that to say?

Morrison came out of himself long enough to light a cigarette.

There's so much you can never know, he said.

Jimmy poured more whiskey into the glass.

What the fuck are you talking about? he said.

You ever think about him trying to sleep when he remembers things? Morrison said.

I don't think about him. I'm just happy when he goes.

The old man's a hero.

He ain't no hero, the bartender said. He's a piece of shit. Why don't he get a bottle and stay home. It would be cheaper. He wouldn't run out of money that way.

He just needs some noise.

There's TV for that, Jimmy said. All those channels to talk you to sleep. It works for me every night.

The bartender left the bottle on the bar and walked off to pull draughts for the firemen who were grab-assing around the table. All of the darts were bent. Jack's warm beer sat on a paper coaster. Morrison drank quietly as if waiting for the Scotch to take his mind even if he knew it would not. They sat together, looking out the barred window, past the neon bar lights, out into the thin sheets of rain, up the flooded gutters with glowing puddles at the traffic light turning from red to green. The wind was blowing straight along the empty street. They could see the yellow fog trailing in the wind.

I love you like a son, Morrison said.

Jack was embarrassed.

Did you ever want your father to say that? Morrison said.

A dead guy can't talk and my old man's always been dead, Jack said.

Morrison drank. His face was wet.

But I'm your father now, he said. I'll even be your sister's father. I'll do right by her.

Jack hid his shaking hands beneath the edge of the bar.

I'll hold that Donny motherfucker, Morrison said. You'll put the barrel of my .38 against his head.

Just to scare him? Jack said.

Did the gooks scare your old man or kill him? We were fucking their sisters. In the ass, the mouth, between their little gook tits.

*Vietnam ain't my war. It's just a dead father.*

I watched her fuck him, Jack said.

Morrison sat like a piece of statuary between his swallows of Scotch.

I'll teach you to forget about that, he said.

They drank until last call when the cowered shapes of the drinkers became white in the turned up lights. The men stood tightly at the bar like cars parked against a curb and Jimmy pulled their last draughts and took their change from the counter in payment. Morrison was drinking hard, but he was not drunk. The liquor only made his silences longer. He stared at the cracks in the wall, more hollow than tight. The men leaned against the bar on their elbows, waxen and black-toothed, their laughter like the calls of strange birds. Morrison handed Jack the truck keys without looking at him. He smoked pensively and said nothing, perhaps even thinking that he'd spoken. Jack took the keys and walked out the door where the rags of fog made the city vanish and then reappear again.

The rain slackened as Jack turned into the alley that went up behind the bar to where the truck was parked. The garbage had been collected and a few stray beer bottles lay in the puddles. He stopped by the front of the truck, green and marred by rust, then lit a cigarette. The alley came out to a cross street but he could not see that far because of the fog. He thought that maybe the sky had fallen, or the earth had lifted. *Piss on Vietnam and these sad men both dead and alive. It wasn't my war. What I didn't see doesn't have to be in my head.*

The dazed black came from the dark dragging his feet, and the knees of his pants were mud wet from where he had fallen. The rain beat into his head. His face ticked. Jack ignored him and looked for the door key on the ring. The black came closer to the truck, stumbling as if his legs had no bones. Jack watched his image in the window and his long bum's coat turned from the wind. He crouched down to see the tires, the cracked brakelights, the rusted doors with head-sized holes.

I like that cap over the back, he said. It's nice the way it's all closed up like that. Probably keeps you real dry. I bet even drier than a bone.

The man smiled at Jack. The beads of rain trickled down his face, his eyes ran red. He was scant, wispy, surreal in the hue of fog, ragged and wet to his shoes. He reeled up to the truck and put his finger against the fender as if he were figuring the ripeness of fruit.

I'd drive a truck like that all over the city, he said. I'd never stop except for gas. Not even for the womens. I wouldn't give them a ride even if I was going their way. Shit on them. I'd put the law on any bitch that got lippy.

The man was trying to stand straight, grabbing at the sides of his grimy trousers to steady himself. His head hung sideways, almost to his shoulder.

You drive your truck like that? he said.

It's not mine, Jack said.

But you drive it.

No.

I bet you do, the man said. I bet you leave all the womens just standing where they stand. That's the way. The womens I know would make you walk if they was driving. Half your money they get and all the booty they got.

I guess.

It ain't nothing to guess, the man said. I'm a man who knows about the womens.

The man slapped his knee.

You know what I'm going to ask God? he said.

Jack watched him drool.

I'm going to ask Him why He gave me the excitement and no money, the man said. Don't He know no better? All a poor man can do is beat his shit and dream. And then He say spilling seeds is a sin.

Jack flipped his cigarette over the truck and buttoned up his coat and started to open the door. The man stood an arm's length away, his head bobbing without him knowing it.

But I do love all the womens, he said. I'd probably break down and give them all rides. Shit, I'd even be begging them to get inside.

The man staggered toward Jack with scabby eyes and laughed so that his toothless mouth opened. His gums were black and bloody, white froth in his lip corners. He slapped the air from the laughter, then collapsed forward into Jack's arms. Their cheeks touched and puffs of sour breath were exchanged between their faces. Jack grabbed him by the shoulders and stood him straight but his rickety legs gave way.

Go easy, Jack said.

But that truck keep you dry, the man said. If you're wet, you don't have to stay that way. Not in that truck.

They faced each other like slow dancers and breathed cold. Jack was moving the man toward the telephone pole and the dumpster when his legs gave way altogether. He was caught off balance while the man vomited on his face and they fell backward against the truck door. The man looked at him like a ventriloquist's dummy, coughing up hard from his stomach, spitting bubbles of blood and vomit, green black phlegm. His laughter never stopped.

Jack was leaning backward into the sideview mirror and trying to press the man off of him. He steadied himself and panted and looked up. The blurred city lights hung over the streets like a dawn eternally waiting to break. The man's eyeballs were lost somewhere in his forehead. His eye whites turned blood-red. A dazed happy smile passed across his mouth. Jack gritted his teeth, took hold of the man's shoulders, and pushed him to his feet when Morrison came out of the fog, running through the puddles like a dog upon prey. The pistol was palmed in his hand and it fell three times against the man's skull before Jack had found his balance. Morrison steamed cold breath, his face darker than the night, as if without eyes. The man's legs bowed and buckled and his shoulders fell from Jack's hands. Morrison showed his teeth and followed the body down, caving the head with the gunmetal. Jack was paralyzed while the open skull slid along his chest and stomach, the blood pulsing from the wound the way wax drips from a candle. Then Morrison fired. The bullet struck the man in the neck and the body flattened with a sucking moan.

The ex-cop held the pistol ready while a flock of pigeons landed in the alley and hopped on line through the fog. His eyes cast about wildly. Morrison kicked the man's head to see if he was dead. It opened horribly. His boot toe came away wet. Jack gasped and looked up the alley. Past dark houses. Empty lots. Rusted chainlink fences covered with wind-blown trash. His breathing quickened, and he stood teetering, staring through tears.

It wasn't that way, Jack said. It wasn't like you saw it.

Morrison shoved the pistol in his belt and opened the truck cap while the pigeons fanned out to scavenge, cooing darkly. He straddled the dead man.

Grab him up under the shoulders, he said.

Jack went to run away, but Morrison seized his thick wrist and looked over into his face, his lightless eyes like water in darkness. Jack flailed and kicked and tried to pull away. He called out to the pigeons as if they were the men of his old rifle platoon but there was nothing save the pigeons and the rags of fog. He strained against Morrison's hold like a leashed dog, drawing his arm until it was perfectly straight.

The ex-cop pulled him close.

I told you to grab him up, he said.

Jack twisted about. He looked for the pigeons but they were gone.

Grab him, Morrison said.

Jack was crying. Morrison talked to him the way he'd talk to a dog and after a while Jack stopped pulling and stood very still. He fell backward against the truck and heaved beer. Then Morrison turned loose of his wrist and waited. Jack sensed the ex-cop's shadow cast over him, but he would not look up. *I am lost. I am lost right with him.*

Morrison sped up the alley past the lighted cross street then back into the dark, still speeding. Then he turned hard out onto Jackson so that the body, shrouded in a wool blanket, rolled against the fire walls of the truck bed, before he slowed on the wet asphalt, passed the closed restaurants and the idling bus on Halsted, then turned onto the flooded potholes of Des Plaines Avenue and accelerated past the vague contours of Saint Patrick's Cathedral half hidden in the fog. The storm clouds were infused with city light and rolled across the sky like the current from a vast river. Jack was sitting close against the door, as if he would jump out at the next stoplight. The ex-cop wore no coat because it became bloody from the man's head when they lifted his sagged body into the truck bed. His eyes were unblinking and bore straight ahead. Jack saw his face in the lights from an oncoming semi, then it was dark, then he saw his face exactly as they came out onto Roosevelt Road. The street was ripped up by a backhoe and men were working on a gas main by the light from portable flood lamps. Morrison's face was white and the iron cold of his eyes showed in the bright light from the lamps.

The night was dark again when Morrison pulled onto the Dan Ryan Expressway, and the fog congealed the highway lights. His teeth were clenched beneath tight lips. They headed south toward Watega County and the brown river of Jack Tyne's youth where the roily current would become the grave for this unknown dead man slumped among toolboxes and empty J&B bottles. In the sideview mirror, Jack watched the skyline recede into the fog before disappearing altogether as if it had never been at all.

The rain had lulled when they left the city and came into a flooded plain of wrecked fields; the clouds had moved along the sky but the fog remained like a bad smell. The storms were following them down south, looming thunderheads coursing in the winds. Morrison steered the truck and stared ahead with his way of looking that made Jack wonder if he saw out of his own eyes. He had been stealing glances into them. Morrison's eyes had different depths and sometimes they seemed wide and lit so that Jack thought he could see into the man and know him, but now they were rock dead. In the window glass his reflection was rimmed by Morrison's own. He stared out at the familiar country. The illusion of the furrow lines in the swamped fields spun like cycle wheels with their passing. The hedge branches thrashed violently in the wind. They sat now like the two strangers that they were.

He was standing there, Jack said. That was all. He liked your truck and then collapsed.

You think so? Morrison said.

I know. It wasn't the way you saw it.

He was just like the nigger you took a walk with the night I found you?

Blake wasn't like that.

You know it all, don't you?

Jack was silent.

There's more to this asshole world than your sister's tits, Morrison said.

It just wasn't the way you saw it.

Jack was listening to the tires spin on the wet asphalt when Morrison grabbed his neck and squeezed. The truck swerved across the lane while the heavy rains came suddenly upon the dark land, then straightened out again between the road lines. Morrison's hand was hot and calloused and wet. Jack offered no resistance. *I've had my chances to run. Goddamn all my watching.* Morrison pushed his face into the window around their overlapping reflections and the glass bowed outward against his nose and his nose popped and opened and leaked hot smears of blood. His vision went blacker than the night. His face slid down the glass and his head slumped awkwardly, chin to chest. Morrison lifted his face to show Jack himself in the window.

I gave you life, Morrison said.

Jack slumped crying against the door when Morrison let go of his neck. The blood was mottled on the glass and dripped through his fogged breath. He held his nose and caught the blood with his cupped hand. He could still feel Morrison's hand strange and brutal upon his neck, but now the ex-cop was driving quietly. Beyond his profile the clouds passed in the eastern sky like continents from another planet. The dome of the moon showed perfectly white through a break in the overcast before vanishing behind a bank of darker clouds.

Morrison drove down off the interstate in the rain when they came into Watega County and over the plain of washed fields where to the west the General Foods plant billowed white smoke as if it were smoldering ruins. Grayish water filled the bar ditches so that the narrow road held water like a channel and the bald truck tires splashed loudly through the submerged blacktop. Jack directed Morrison laconically while the rain created the illusion of moving walls. They crossed the broad Watega River bounded by a line of trees. The trees were a deep black in the gray night, and their twisted branches stretched over the flood crest and left diffuse shadows on the roily water. Thunderheads gathered to the east and quick flashes of lightning illumed barns caved beneath tin roofs, fencelines drowned to the middle strand of barbed wire. The town was across acres of ruined fields, the lights from the taverns and clapboard woodframes and grocery stores smeared by the wall of rain.

Jack pointed out the turns and only spoke the direction. Morrison responded by driving them down half-washed tractor roads toward the river bottom. Jack sneezed thin splatters of blood into his hands. The wind was beating violently through the trees and in the wind were spinning sticks. He watched lightning far to the west over the streets and trailer courts of town and wondered vaguely if his mother was watching these same thin wires in the sky. The country was wasted and he tried to feel many things for it, but all his memories here were now dark shadows, their old power over him gone, as if beaten in fight by Morrison's slag eyes and the body that rolled against the toolboxes with every turn. He was left to the dark water and the nights of these storms forever to come because he knew his soul was true in aspect with them. The time in his life had passed when he could think himself a better man than he was and console his mind with thoughts about how he should be and how he should feel. Now there was only what he was, a sad man who returned his sadness back upon the world as if a blackjack dealer turning cards.

The rain lulled, and there was a sudden lifting of the fog. Morrison cut the headlights and drove along the trackless road heading for a line of hardwoods that marked the Watega River. In the bottom fields the night was waiting there sedated for them. When the moonwash hit Morrison's eyes, they smoldered like the ashes of a dream. Jack felt the cold and shivered.

Branches slid along the side windows with slow give before straightening back into the wet night. The truck went down an incline along the field, fishtailed out of the flooded ruts, and slid slantwise until it stalled. The alternator light flashed from the speedometer. Morrison was silent, his face lost to the hedge shadows. He turned the engine and it took four tries before the starter caught and the tires freed from the deep mud. He drove up to the woods, the tree bark white from the moon, then shut down the engine and stared across the steaming hood. He chewed on nothing.

Jack stepped from the truck without being told. His nose blood had melted on his hands from the moisture of the night. Morrison nodded at him from across the hood. The steam was gone. They stood a while as if the last men in a world gone to mud. Morrison turned up his shirt collar against the damp wind and looked out at the black woods and the river beyond them before walking back behind the truck. His shadow was beneath him in the ankle-deep water like a drowned soul.

Morrison had the cap and gate of the truck open before Jack worked his way through the sludge. The clouds were mounting up from the east and the dark now upon them came in a sudden closing of the sky and snuffed the moonlight and the shadows it cast. Jack stood wincing in the wind while Morrison took hold of the man's ankles as if they were plow handles. The misshapen head struck tool boxes and coils of rope and the gate itself before the whole body came weightless into the night. Morrison let go of the legs and let the body drop to the mud. It was still wrapped in a blanket as it made an imprint and sank. The head slipped free, and it was too dark to see the red blood, but the wounds shone. Jack reeled back against the muddy cap window. Morrison stood over the body and filled the tool-boxes and worked easily and with method before latching them closed. He pulled them to the edge of the gate.

Get his clothes off, he said. They'll hold air in the water and this nigger will float all the way to New Orleans. The fucking animal.

Jack stared at the head slumped in the mud. The bullet holes gored the neck and the skull. There were clotted gashes from the pistol whipping. He knew the man would have no face or throat and that come daylight, the truck would be a welter of blood.

Morrison shoved a rusty hatchet into his belt and slung two coils of rope over his shoulder. He turned to see that Jack had not moved. When Jack and Morrison met eyes, a wind blew from the black trees down into the bottom fields. The ex-cop held a hunting knife.

I always fucking tell you things, he said.

The ex-cop pushed Jack away with his hand and Jack closed his eyes when he kicked the blanket off the body.

Morrison bent down and the knife ripped through the man's coat and shirt and the cold rain fell slant upon them and tapped in the water. When Jack opened his eyes, the man lay naked in the shell of his clothes as if an enormous nightcrawler driven from its hole by the rain. His white eyes stared up from beneath the muddy water. Morrison pointed a homemade knife at Jack that he'd found on the body, a sharpened gutter nail with a tape handle.

You know what this is? he said.

Jack looked at this bleak man and the dark trees behind him.

You even got a fucking idea what it is? he said.

Yes.

You'd of had this thing up under your ribs. The asshole was waiting.

Morrison demonstrated how it could have happened, stabbing into the air, then threw the knives into the truck and closed the gate.

Jack did not watch Morrison lift the body from the water before they set off through the field toward the woods. He only slung the coils of rope and took up the toolboxes that would weight the man to the river bottom, then led the way along a broken slat fence and dwarfed cornstalks and the thin trees that rose from the mud like deformed bodies. Morrison slogged quietly through the water behind him. The sky was leaden with the hard rain to come.

The night of the woods hung darker than the night of the fields. The mist was heavy and cold and hard to breathe. He and Morrison did not speak; the ex-cop was only bootfalls in the leaf mulch. They walked along the rocky trail that went up the berm. Jack heard the river before he saw it, a dull rush that quieted the noise they made through these woods. They crested the bluff and blew cold. When he saw the river, he did not think it was the river at all, but a long piece of fallen night. This was not the Watega River that he remembered with slow eddy water swirling around small islands and the limestone bluffs

along the banks where swallows nested. The trees on the
far bank were drowned to their crowns and the current
moved without discernible motion, the bluffs beneath the
water. The river was more like a dark slough. The water
rose back into the woods and stagnated in a final blackness
between the wind beats that riffled the surface and threw
the raindrops back at the night.

The moon was gone into the clouds when they made it
through the flooded woods to the river's edge, bitter and
sodden beneath the wrecked sky where it was raining
again: a small cold autumnal rain. The naked man hung
off Morrison's shoulder at the waist and his long, thin
arms dangled almost to the mud. His fingers were open.
The bullet holes in his throat dripped mist and blood.
Dead leaves stuck to what remained of his head and his
rib cage was pronounced through his coal skin as if he'd
been a man who would rather drink than eat. Morrison
spat. He looked at the sky. He leaned sideways and the
body fell from his shoulder to lie curled in the muck beside a waterworn log. The man was no more a man than
the deadheads jammed against the tree trunks, the broken
wire fences that separated the fields.

Jack was watching the far bank for birds when Morrison took the hatchet from his belt and stood over the body.
He breathed quietly in the cold air and looked at Jack. The
two of them were just standing there. There was no wind
but Jack knew that one was gathering across the river by
the sway of the trees. He found he was still holding the
toolboxes and the rope and he dropped it all in the mud.
The water seeped into his boots.

Morrison stared at the hatchet in his hand, the blade
dripping rain. All animation had left his face as if the
thoughts in him just died. He was little more than the
corpse he stood over. No more a man than it. No more a
soul than the fog. He was beyond it all when he looked at
Jack, his eyes almost floating.

Get out of here, he said.

Jack did not move. He wiped his face with his coat sleeve.

This is where we end, Jack Tyne. It's all shit. I hope you're better with the memories than I was.

We can just leave now, Jack said.

You don't mean it.

I do.

We never leave anything. Never.

That was all. The ex-cop turned his back to Jack, then knelt down in the mud and pulled the man's head over the log. The legs were under muddy water. There was no sound save the mounting wind. Jack Tyne took his last look at Morrison while the ex-cop lifted the hatchet into the night, then vanished off into the thicket, gone the way he was found, slewed up in mud past his knees, wallowing along the berm with outstretched hands to push the woodvine and brownbrier away from his face. When he ran he did not turn to look at Morrison again. In the darkness he knew there would be nothing left to see.

**M**orrison's hands were hot with blood and blood ran down his cheeks like sweat. The body slid headless off the log and lay with the crooked sticks in the mud. He stood with the hatchet and pitched the head into the river long after Jack's boots stopped sucking in the mud, and walked to the water's edge and then into the water itself where he stood thigh deep. The rings were fading from the splash the head made. A flotsam of dead leaves and weeds went past his waist. He looked up at the paling moonlight and he looked down the river. The twisted tree shapes rose from the flood like lightning-struck men. The river was darker than all the nights of his life and it reflected nothing. Not the trees. Not even his own broken shadow. He dropped the hatchet from his hand and surveyed the country until he forgot that the boy had ever been.

He took the pistol from his belt and cocked the hammer to lighten the trigger pull and then raised it above his head. He walked out into the water. A cold wind was coming across the river. It was gusting down from the darkening shapes of cloud all along the horizon where the fields curved downward as if meeting the final edge of land and it was crossing bleak and raw through the river trees. His boots sank in the mire of the river bottom but he kept walking until the wavelets shot water into his mouth. He closed his eyes amid this noise. *No man in this life ever gets any better than what he is.*

**T**he rains came without thunder and fell in black sheets after the pistol shot sounded from down the river. The Watega exploded into thousands of bubbles. The wind sent large swells back into the treeline where Jack ran even though he knew he was not being chased. Morrison had come to this river to begin his long dream beneath the dark water. The hard rain drove past Jack's eyes and he ran into it and lost all direction as if he were spinning through the woods with the sticks. He shivered from many things but not the cold. He was guilty of the same blood that Morrison drew and inside him were the black dreams of cowards who drew blood by the very act of turning away. His eyes were blinded by the rain and he cursed and cast about for direction.

The woodvine cuffed his throat like it was Morrison arisen from the river to pull him back.

He ran deeper into the rain, without aim, as if a man tumbling. Dead trees were heaped and crossed beneath the water and they caught his ankle and tripped him. The fall was fast and he did not know he was falling until a log opened his forehead. The blood ran down his face and he could taste it with the cold rain.

The two deer appeared on the slope of the ridge to watch him cast about in the water. There was a buck with ten points and his small doe. The wind blew rain about their erect shapes. He could see the steam rising from their noses like hot logs and he could see that they stood on dry ground with wide eyes and stiff necks. They held eyes for a long minute, tiny rings of light in the wet darkness. The water rose past his chest. He tried standing but his ankles were tangled with the deadfall while a wind burst from across the river and made waves that rose over his head. He swallowed water. Soon the deer turned and sauntered off sleekly through the rain and the timber. He whistled for the deer but they were gone. He whistled and whistled, sitting in the undying darkness where there was no sound anywhere save the water lapping the hickory trunks. Then he stopped. He touched his gashed forehead and bowed his head and held his face in his hands and cried. He wept for a long while and did not know that in time the rain would cease and the dawn would pale the eastern sky, as it had yesterday, for one man and for all men.

# Also from
# AKASHIC BOOKS

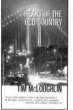

*Heart of the Old Country* by Tim McLoughlin
"*Heart of the Old Country* is a wise and tender first novel, though its youthful narrator would surely not like to hear that said. His boisterous, irreverent, often hilarious tough-guy pose is his armor, for he comes from the heart of old Brooklyn, where compassion and emotion are considered fatal weaknesses. Yet underneath it all, he shows a love for humanity so deep it might equal Dostoevksy's. Tim McLoughlin is a master storyteller inthe tradition of such great New York City writers as Hubert Selby Jr. and Richard Price. I can't wait for his second book!"
–Kaylie Jones, author of *A Soldier's Daughter Never Cries*
216 pages, trade paperback; $14.95
ISBN: 1-888451-15-7

*Adios Muchachos* by Daniel Chavarría
"Daniel Chavarría has long been recognized as one of Latin America's finest writers. Now he again proves why with *Adios Muchachos*, a comic mystery peopled by a delightfully mad band of miscreants, all of them led by a woman you will not soon forget–Alicia, the loveliest bicycle whore in all Havana."
–Edgar Award-winning author William Heffernan
245 pages, paperback; $13.95
ISBN: 1-888451-16-5

*Michael* by Henry Flesh
(**1999 Lambda Literary Award Winner**)
*with illustrations by John H. Greer*
"Henry's the king. He writes with incessant crispness. Sex is reluctantly juicy, life is reluctant and winning–even when his characters lose. What's it all about, Henry? I think you know."
–Eileen Myles, author of *Cool For You*
120 pages, trade paperback; $12.95
ISBN: 1-888451-12-2

*Kamikaze Lust* by Lauren Sanders
"Like an official conducting an all-out strip search, first-time novelist Lauren Sanders plucks and probes her characters' minds and bodies to reveal their hidden lusts, and when all is said and done, nary a body cavity is spared."
–*Time Out New York*
287 pages, trade paperback; $14.95
ISBN: 1-888451-08-4

*Manhattan Loverboy* by Arthur Nersesian
(author of *The Fuck-Up*)
"Nersesian's newest novel is paranoid fantasy and fantastic comedy in the service of social realism, using the methods of L. Frank Baum's *Wizard of Oz* or Kafka's *The Trial* to update the picaresque urban chronicles of Augie March, with a far darker edge . . ." –*Downtown Magazine*
203 pages, paperback; $13.95
ISBN: 1-888451-09-2

*Once There Was a Village* by Yuri Kapralov
"If there were a God, then *Once There Was a Village*, Yuri Kapralov's chronicle of life as an exiled Russian artist on the Lower East Side, would have gone to Broadway instead of *Rent*. Only the staging of this book, set amid the riots of the late '60s and the crime-infested turmoil of the early '70s, might look like a cross between *Les Miserables* and *No Exit*." –*Village Voice*
163 pages, trade paperback; $12.00
ISBN: 1-888451-05-X

*The Big Mango* by Norman Kelley
"Want a scathing social and political satire? Look no further than Kelley's second effort featuring 'bad girl' African-American PI and part-time intellectual Nina Halligan–it's X-rated, but a romp of a read . . . Nina's acid takes on recognizable public figures and institutions both amuse and offend . . . Kelley spares no one, blacks and whites alike, and this provocative novel is sure to attract attention . . . " –*Publisher's Weekly*
270 pages, trade paperback; $14.95
ISBN: 1-888451-10-6

---

These books are available at local bookstores. They can also be purchased with a credit card online through www.akashicbooks.com. To order by mail, send a check or money order to:

**Akashic Books**
**PO Box 1456**
**New York, NY 10009**
**www.akashicbooks.com**
**Akashic7@aol.com**

(Prices include shipping. Outside the U.S., add $3 to each book ordered.)